THE LO

ED

Ed Gorman became a full-time writer after twenty years in advertising, and is acknowledged as being one of the worlds leading writers of dark suspense. He is the founder and editor of Mystery Scene and lives in Cedar Rapids, Iowa with his wife, novelist Carol Graham. Amongst his other novels are *Cage of Night*, *Night Kills*, *Serpent's Kiss* and *The Poker Club*.

Praise For Ed Gorman

"Books like this are what inspired me to become a writer in the first place." —DEAN R KOONTZ

"Gorman has a way of getting into his characters, and they have a way of getting into you" — ROBERT BLOCH, author of *Psycho*

"Gorman pulls things off with sleek bravura, reclaiming the field from the legions of cardboard cutout serial killers" — TIME OUT

Other Titles by Ed Gorman

Serpent's Kiss
The Poker Club
Night Kills
Cage Of Night
New Improved Murder

Ed Gorman

THE LONG MIDNIGHT

CT Publishing

First published in Great Britain by CT Publishing, 1999.

This edition 1999 CT Publishing.

A CIP catalogue record for this book is
available from the British Library.

ISBN 1-902002-08-3

9 8 7 6 5 4 3 2 1

Book design and typography by DP Fact & Fiction.
Printed and bound in Great Britain by Caledonian
International Book Manufacturing, Bishopbriggs, Glasgow.

To Pat LoBrutto: a great editor, a fine friend.

Tom Owens spent many hours going through the third and fourth drafts of this manuscript. I thank him for his help.
—Ed Gorman

THE LONG MIDNIGHT

RICHARD CANDELMAS was sixteen years old before anyone discovered his secret.

On a fall day when leaves tore from the trees and skittered against the windows of Woodrow Wilson High, Mrs Craig turned suddenly from the blackboard to face her class. She looked pale and shaky, as if she had just been taken ill.

She staggered a few feet to her desk, the history book she'd been holding dropping to the floor.

Mary Louise Allbright, the school's number one brown-nose, hurried to the front of the room and helped the teacher to her chair.

By now Mrs Craig appeared to be gasping for air. "Water," she managed to say.

Mary Louise grabbed Mrs Craig's drinking cup and flew from the room and returned moments later, silver water spilling from the cup as she rushed it to the teacher.

The students were whispering among themselves... What was going on here? Was the beautiful blonde Mrs Craig having some sort of attack? The boys especially hoped not, because half of them had a crush on the woman, Richard Candelmas included.

After taking a few sips of water, and drawing air deep into her lungs, Mrs Craig appeared to be better. "I'm sorry if I frightened you, class. I just got—dizzy."

But her problems weren't over yet.

A violent spasm passed through Mrs Craig's fetching body and she grasped the desk for support. Several of the students now wondered if they were witnessing their first epileptic seizure. They hoped not.

"Maybe I should dismiss class early today," Mrs Craig said tentatively, her voice and manner still weak. "Just keep on reading about the Civil War. Again, I'm sorry if I frightened any of you."

The students muttered various kinds of get-wells and started shuffling out of the classroom—most of them trying to hide the absolute elation they felt over being dismissed early. Elation wouldn't look too good considering Mrs Craig's shaky condition.

As Richard Candelmas rose from his seat and started down the aisle, Mrs Craig raised her head and looked directly at him. "Richard, I'd like you to stay a few minutes if you don't mind."

The students around him smirked as they usually did whenever Candelmas appeared or was mentioned. A tall, gangly boy with sad but spooky dark eyes, Candelmas lived on the edge of town in the type of tin shack that was a holdover from the Depression—it had ended only six years ago, at the start of World War II. The kids called him Scarecrow because, in fact, he resembled one, raw bones seeming to jut out of his ragged clothes; a figure that managed to be both pathetic and menacing at the same time.

Candelmas suspected why Mrs Craig had asked him to stay after class. He was terrified. Nobody, not even his old man, had suspected his secret until this very afternoon.

As he waited for the teacher to speak, Candelmas glanced around the room at the American flag standing in the corner, the portrait of George Washington hanging to the left of the blackboard, and, on a small dais, the plump orange jack-o-lantern that Mrs Craig had carved and brought to school.

After the last student had left, Mrs Craig said, "Why don't you go close the door, Richard, and then come back here?"

He kept trying to read her voice. Was it anger he heard? Fear? Both?

He did as she asked.

She looked at him, still pale and trembling, and said, "I know what you did this afternoon."

He said nothing, just stared at her.

"I'm almost afraid to say it because it will sound so crazy and so silly."

He still said nothing.

"How long have you been doing it, Richard?"

He shrugged. "I guess I don't know what you're talking about, Mrs Craig."

She was so beautiful; he was always shy around her.

"It's a new world now, Richard," Mrs Craig said. "Last year we defeated the Germans and the Japanese, and now we're talking about developing all the things we learned about in the

10

war—jet aeroplanes and atomic power and things like that." She gazed at him steadily. "The world is probably even ready for people like you."

Richard dropped his gaze, stiff and uncertain of what to do or say.

"Have you always been able to do this, Richard?"

He surprised himself by answering her question honestly. "Yes."

She sighed. "When I realised what was happening, I got scared. I wasn't really sick or anything I was just—frightened. That's when I started getting faint and began trembling and—"

"I'm sorry, Mrs Craig."

"Oh, don't be sorry, Richard! My Lord, be glad that you have your abilities. I'm sure there are other people like you in the world. You'll be able to help mankind enormously, once we figure out how to use your—skills." She raised her cup and sipped water. She set it back down and folded her hands primly before her. She had a very kissable mouth. "Do you know where the State University is?"

"Sure. In Bridgeport."

"Yes. There's a doctor there named Redstone. I'd like you to meet him."

"How come?"

"Just to talk. I'd like to describe to him what happened to me—to us—this afternoon. And then I'd like you to tell him about yourself." She paused and said, "Now that gas rationing has been lifted, I'd be willing to drive us. I can call Cliff—Dr Redstone is a friend of my husband's—and tell him we're coming over tomorrow morning. I'll ask your father's permission, of course. How would that be?"

"Fine. I guess."

"You sound afraid, Richard."

"Well, you know."

"He's a very nice man."

"I know. But—" He shrugged.

She smiled. She seemed to sense her power over him. There was just a hint of the seductive in her smile. At least as Candelmas

11

saw it.

He turned to look out the window at the scattering autumn leaves and the cold grey sky. It would snow soon, perhaps as early as tonight. Candelmas, as always, felt very much alone.

"Could you meet me here at school tomorrow morning at eight o'clock?" Mrs Craig said.

"I guess."

"I'll buy us a nice breakfast and a nice lunch. We'll have a pleasant time tomorrow. I promise." She could not keep the excitement from her voice. Her deep blue eyes conveyed excitement, too. She looked at Richard as if he were a new and wonderful gift. "See you then, Richard."

Candelmas didn't leave at first. He stood there wanting to tell her some things. About the headaches he had sometimes... about the nightmares... about the feeling that his strange gifts made him a freak. About how lonely he was.

But he could see that she would want to hear none of it.

She was excited about his gifts and didn't want to hear anything negative.

He wanted to talk to her but he knew it would be like bringing bad news to somebody's birthday party.

Quietly, in his awkward way, Scarecrow left Mrs Craig's room.

Though school had started in late August, Candelmas hadn't gone until October. Even with the war over, there were a lot of soldiers to be fed, so the government allowed some kids to help with the harvest and put off their schooling for a time. Candelmas had spent September picking four-hundred-pound half-sacks of spuds a day; for this he was paid six cents a half-sack. This gave him enough to buy food for his father and himself. Even now, two or three times a week after school, Candelmas pitched hay and hauled beans, occasionally getting to sit up on one of the new self-propelled combines that threshed grain so neatly. Candelmas enjoyed standing in the middle of the field on a nice sunny autumn day, the tang of apples and smoky leaves like an incredible perfume, nobody around to smirk or snicker when he came into a room, no old man to curse him and bat him around.

But directly after leaving Mrs Craig's room, Candelmas knew that he would no longer enjoy the luxury of being by himself in farm fields, at least not in fields around here.

His secret had been discovered. He had to get out of town and fast.

The tin shack sat next to a winding silver creek. Outside it was parked an ancient Model-T Ford coupe, the standard black paint half-brown now with rust. Downslope, near the creek itself, was the outhouse where, despite the stench and the buzzing flies, he often sat enjoying himself with used issues of Superman and Captain Marvel as they battled the goose-stepping Krauts and the slant-eyed Japs. Of course, now that the war was over, they'd gone back to fighting standard-issue gangsters who weren't nearly as menacing as Hitler and Hirohito.

Inside the tin shack, he found his old man sleeping in the darkness on the couch. A small radio played a number called 'Tuxedo Junction.'

His mother, who had died of tuberculosis, had left a small battered suitcase behind. Candelmas quickly filled it with his belongings. He topped off the few shirts and pants and socks with the comic books.

Suitcase in hand, he went to stand over his sleeping father. The old man's snoring was oppressive. Every so often he'd cry out a few strangled words from his nightmares, and then fall back to snoring. Standing here staring down at him, Candelmas felt nothing. The man was an alcoholic brute. He'd slapped and punched Candelmas's mother regularly, no matter how many times Candelmas raised his fists in her defence. Candelmas, knowing this would be the last time he ever saw his father, wanted to feel something—one iota of remorse for leaving, or sentiment for being his blood son. But in his heart there was—nothing.

But something compelled him to shake the old man awake and he was abruptly staring down into the sad red eyes of a drunkard. "I wanted to say good-bye."

"Just where the hell do you think you're going?"

"That doesn't matter."

The old man struggled to sit up, pitched his legs over the side of the couch, dragged out a Lucky butt and lit it. He hacked for a long minute. "It's because of that crazy shit you do, ain't it?" The old man grinned with bad teeth. "You think I don't know what you do? Get into my mind sometimes; push little things around with just your thoughts." The old man shook his head. "Your ma did stuff like that, too."

Candelmas was startled by this news. His mother?

"Maybe that's what killed her so young," the old man said. "You ever think of that?" Then the old man's grizzled face grew hard. "I'm glad yer leavin'. I didn't like that queer shit in her and I don't like it any better in you. It ain't right. It ain't right at all."

And with that, the old man lay back down on the couch and promptly started snoring again. Candelmas wondered if the old man would even remember this conversation in the morning. He seldom remembered anything these days. Candelmas took the Lucky from his old man's fingers and stubbed it out in an ashtray.

Candelmas left, closing the door on the tin shack for the last time.

At midnight, Candelmas stood on an empty stretch of two-lane highway ninety miles west of the Nebraska border. He had walked twenty-seven miles thus far. But freezing rain and weary bones took their toll, so now he hitchhiked, his thumb up defiantly in the darkness.

Suddenly the baleful eyes of a produce truck peered through the falling silver rain. Squeaking brakes told Candelmas that at last he had a ride. The trucker took him all the way to Chicago, where next afternoon Candelmas caught a bus to New York. Candelmas wondered if the truck driver had any idea who he would someday be. In his heart, Candelmas was already a great man; now he had to set about convincing the world of that fact.

New York City in mid-1940s was even more overwhelming than Candelmas had expected. He spent the first eighteen hours off the Greyhound just wandering around, especially along the electric spectacle of Broadway. He stood in the shadows watching Packard limousines pull up to the kerb and liveried servants holding doors for elegant people who seemed to belong to a race or species that was somehow superior to mere mortals. He had never seen women so beautiful and erotic, nor men so handsome and arrogant.

He liked to take the ferry ride so he could see Manhattan at night, the glowing eyes of the skyscraper windows, the silver spires of building tops that seemed to tear holes in the midnight sky. Easy to imagine the Batman of comic books moving about in this Gotham of shadow and full golden moon shining on gutter and gala alike.

He spent three nights sleeping in a hotel that seemed to have no name other than FIREPROOF ROOMS 25 CENTS A NIGHT. He saw a wino in the communal bathroom puke up blood and listened as a nervous young man asked if he wanted to be 'friends.' He left the nervous young man quickly.

He spent the days in the Bronx branch of the New York Public Library. The fine architecture and interior design was just as overpowering as Broadway had been. He told the woman at the reference desk that he wanted to learn all he could about the stock market.

She glanced at him sceptically but pointed him to the proper sections.

Over the next few days he began to understand how Wall Street worked. The requirements for getting a stock listed on the New York Stock Exchange were staggering and had been so ever since Black Friday, when the stock market had crashed and helped bring on the Depression.

He learned about unlisted securities and fluctuation and getting a quotation and reading a stock ticker. He learned about bull markets and bear markets and buying a seat and odd-lot dealers. He learned about floor brokers and commission houses and over-the-counter trading.

He learned enough, he felt, to put his plan into action.

A week later he was working as a busboy in a private men's club off Wall Street. In the deep leather chairs around the crackling fireplace, and at the elegant tables in the dining room, sat some of the richest and most powerful men in the country.

He spent two weeks there before anything happened.

One afternoon, cleaning off a table, he began frantically looking around the dining room.

He wasn't sure which person it was. The dapper man with the walrus moustache? The liver-spotted one with the mane of white hair? The dashing younger man in the blue suit?

But finally he saw a man looking directly at him and knew immediately that this was the one. The man wasn't sure yet why he was staring at Candelmas. He just had some vague notion that something had changed in his mind. Something *different* was going on here. The man looked startled and slightly afraid.

Candelmas had no idea if the man was a good choice or not. He'd just have to wait and see.

In a few minutes the man was joined by two companions. They began talking right away about business.

Candelmas, whose shift had already ended, locked himself in a dark storage closet and scribbled words on a notepad. *Merger. Make a killing. If we move this afternoon before anybody else finds out about it.*

In all, Candelmas stayed in the storage closet for four-five minutes before the three men got up and left. Candelmas then hurried to a telephone. He had already selected a brokerage, one he'd judged, by the size of its ad in the Yellow Pages, to be small and perhaps even failing.

After some arguing with the receptionist, he was put through to a Mr Feeny.

He quickly laid out the deal for Mr Feeny. He said Feeny could either go along or hang up. Mr Feeny exercised his rights as an American citizen and slammed the phone down. He had elected not to use Candelmas's tip about Empire Airlines.

In the morning, *The Wall Street Journal* reported the entire story. Empire Airlines was being sold to a group of investors that included Howard Hughes. An unnamed source had yesterday bought up a great deal of Empire stock. 'Insider trading' was whispered.

"You could have been a millionaire today, Mr Feeny," Candelmas said when the cranky receptionist put him through to her boss the following day.

"Just who the hell are you and what kind of game are you playing?" Feeny asked.

Later that afternoon, in Feeny's modest offices, Candelmas explained it all. Feeny didn't pretend to understand what Candelmas was talking about. All he knew was that Candelmas had been right about Empire Airlines and might well be right again about other stocks.

He listened, and in the end he sceptically agreed to go along.

By the time he was twenty-one, Candelmas was a millionaire many times over. He was also the captain of busboys in the same private club. His only extravagance was a nice apartment and a new 1951 Admiral TV set with a giant eleven-inch screen.

By now John Feeny had become a major player on Wall Street. He was driven to and from work every day in a private limousine, and *Forbes* and *Time* and *The Wall Street Journal* constantly asked the questions *How does he do it?* and *How long can John Feeny's luck last?*

Candelmas and Feeny did not especially care for each other—Candelmas saw Feeny as shallow, and Feeny, good Yale man that he was, saw Candelmas as strange and in some ways barbaric—but they both needed each other so they honoured their bargain.

Until the day, five years into their partnership, when Candelmas asked Feeny for an accounting. Candelmas had a specific goal, and when his funds equated that amount, he planned to return to the Midwest and go on with his work. He assumed he was near reaching his goal, yet when Feeny told him how much he was worth, Candelmas saw that Feeny had been cheating him all along.

Over lunch, Feeny and his people gone, Candelmas went into the office and transferred money from several office

17

accounts to a Candelmas account in an Ohio bank. The transfer totalled upward of eleven million dollars.

Candelmas then wrote Feeny a letter. *If you hadn't got greedy, I would have made you even richer. But you betrayed my principles and our agreement. Don't try to contact me. If you do, I'll go to the press with the whole story and your Wall Street career will be over— you may even wind up in prison.* He signed it simply *Candelmas*.

Two years later, outside Chicago, a huge estate was fashioned out of timberland. The sprawling main house was built of native stone and ran to forty-eight rooms, with enormous swimming pools built in the east and west wings respectively. To the north was a landing strip for aeroplanes of considerable size. To the south lay a horse ranch. The entire estate was protected by electric fencing and patrolled in military jeeps by armed guards. To pay for all this, Candelmas had started doing business again, though with a more trustworthy Wall Street partner this time.

Soon after the estate was completed, men and women from around the world began visiting Candelmas's place. They flew in and out on one of Candelmas's three private planes and sometimes stayed for as long as three or four months at a time. The estate staff was constantly baffled. Who were these people and what was going on here? Eventually a handful of these people returned to the estate, and stayed permanently. They were assigned rooms in the smaller house that lay a quarter mile from the main house. The staff still had no idea who they were or what they were doing. They all met every day in Candelmas's basement, which had been set up very much like a vast classroom, with desks and blackboards. The only thing lacking was students.

In 1956, following one of his extended and mysterious trips, Candelmas brought a young woman back to the estate. She was lovely in her frail blonde way. Candelmas announced that she was his wife.

Nine months to the day of her appearance, the woman bore

a child. There was great festivity. Nobody could ever remember seeing Candelmas this happy. Ordinarily he was a quiet and solitary man.

Over the next six years, however, Candelmas's happiness with his daughter diminished. Clearly, he loved her and wanted to be a good father, yet it was equally clear that she had disappointed him in some way. He often took her to the basement where the men and women in medical smocks questioned her and gave her tests, but always, always they shook their heads no when Candelmas inquired about her. For all her golden beauty, for all her genuine sweetness, she was, it seemed, a quite ordinary child.

When the girl was six, Candelmas sent both her and her mother away. The word was that he set them up nicely in Connecticut, which was where the mother had been raised. Servants wondered in whispers what kind of man could send his daughter and wife away and never bother to phone or write them.

Not long after, the girl and her mother were killed when their plane crashed into the mountains.

For long months Candelmas was inconsolable; he paid little attention to his work, which was when certain of the scientists he employed began taking effective control of Perpetual Light—the school he had founded for 'special' children—using methods that Candelmas would never have approved. The scientists Candelmas had gathered were given one task: to learn as much as possible about the extrasensory perception of human beings, within the guidelines established by Dr J. B. Rhine at Duke University. Which is what the scientists did. The estate became a repository for every magazine article, every radio interview, every television program, every scholarly speech given on the subject of ESP, and Candelmas's scientists were already exploring ways of improving on Rhine's work, though some of the 'improvements' involved consciousness-expanding drugs and would never have been condoned by Candelmas…

Eventually, almost despite himself, Candelmas began functioning again, but it was whispered that he would never be the same man, as perhaps he wouldn't.

In the spring, when he was thirty-three years old, Candelmas was reading a *Chicago Tribune* article about life in orphanages, when he realised that there was probably a simpler way to achieve his ends.

He called a meeting of his people and discussed his plans. While there were questions, and a few wondered if the randomness of the plan would work, Candelmas, as usual, managed to overpower everybody with his passion.

And Candelmas himself changed: though he used to sleep in late, he was now up at dawn. Where he used to avoid intervening in scientific affairs, he now gave his opinion even when it wasn't sought. And though he used to form his final opinions by consulting others, he now began—after hearing all sides of a given argument —to make such final decisions alone.

He became addicted to TV game shows, even after the scandal of *The $64,000 Question*.

He became a Cubs fan, even though to be such guaranteed a summer-long heartbreak.

He developed a rather sophomoric crush on a former B-movie actress named Susan Cabot, a woman neither all his money nor all his minions could persuade to visit Perpetual Light.

And he implemented his plan.

Throughout the Midwest that spring, as chalky winter turned to blue skies and green grass, Candelmas's long black Packard limousine could be seen pulling up in front of orphanages, and Candelmas himself emerging from the back seat. He was already getting heavier, much in the fashion of the movie director Orson Welles, but his weight only served to make him more imposing.

He had now officially set about trying to conquer the world.

Part One

1

I

WHENEVER MEREDITH SAWYER found herself stuck for a word or a phrase, she rose from her desk and went to look out the window at the spectacle of Chicago. Though she had spent considerable time in New York, San Francisco, and London during her forty-two years, she always came back to her first love, Chicago.

On her return three years ago, the pretty blonde had been doubly lucky. Not only had she found a job as a magazine staff writer—which was her favourite kind of work—it was a magazine that dealt with Chicago history. Her job combined business and pleasure in equal measure.

How she loved to write about the days when ladies wore bustles and men wore homburgs, and Chicago politicians were openly bought and paid for (as opposed to today, when such arrangements were more discreet). Or the world's first Ferris wheel introduced in Chicago in 1893. Or the time the Queen of England visited the city's famous horse auction.

Standing at the window now, she looked at Chicago on this warm, sunny autumn day, the Sears Tower rising proudly into the blue sky, joined by the Wrigley Building, the Tribune Tower, and so many other landmarks.

Today she was writing an article about Mayor Carter Harrison I, who was not only 'colourful' in the accepted sense but who also tolerated vice districts within the city. Many of the city's more proper citizens were outraged. A would-be office seeker ended Harrison's tenure in 1893 by shooting the man dead.

As she looked over the modern skyline stretching to the choppy waters of Lake Michigan, she tried to picture the city as it would have been a hundred years ago —the women in big picture hats and bustles carrying parasols, the men in Edwardian clothing and top hats and muttonchop sideburns standing on

21

the sidewalks talking as horse-drawn hansom cabs and buggies plied the streets. What a romantic time it must have been, and Meredith often enjoyed fanaticising about the era.

Her intercom buzzed. She walked back to her desk, a quietly appealing woman in an inexpensive but fashionably tailored grey suit, her hair drawn back into a loose chignon. She pressed the intercom button.

"Meredith, you've got a visitor."

The voice belonged to Todd Benjamin, *Windy City*'s editor. Todd's calling her meant that the magazine's only other full-time employee, the receptionist-secretary, Sally Clark, was still at lunch.

"All right if I send him in?" Todd said.

Meredith looked at her cluttered office and frowned. She was ordinarily a neat person, but she tended to work in the midst of clutter while she was actually writing. She still used an electric typewriter, and often wadded up pages she hated and scattered them around her tiny space.

"If he thinks he can stand it," she said. A moment later a knock sounded on her door. A man stuck his head inside and said, "I'm Detective Tom Gage with the Chicago Police."

Meredith wasn't sure which surprised her more, Gage's occupation or his melancholy good looks.

As he came into the office, he took out his wallet and showed her his badge. She'd seen this done many times on TV. In person, it was much more effective.

"Mind if I sit down?"

"Please," she said, walking over to the Mr Coffee she kept working all day. "Like a cup?"

"Afraid I've had my quota for the day." He held out a long, graceful hand. It trembled slightly. "I need the caffeine to get going in the morning but it sure takes its toll on my nerves."

She brought her full cup back and sat down. She hoped she wasn't staring too hard at his chiselled face, especially the frank blue eyes that conveyed in equal parts crackling intelligence as well as a real hint of sorrow. He was short, probably could stand to lose fifteen pounds, had dark curly hair that was showing some grey, and appeared to be slightly uneasy in the

22

presence of an attractive woman. But there was something about him—some hint of substance—that Meredith found instantly appealing. He might not be a movie star but he was a damned good-looking man.

"I've never had a visit from a policeman before," she said. "Actually, it's kind of scary."

He smiled. "I wish there were something we could do about that. About scaring people, I mean. But I'm not sure there is. Apparently, most of us learn to be intimidated by authority figures at a very early age. And it stays with us."

"I don't have a bunch of overtime parking tickets built up, do I?" She was only half kidding. She'd heard of people who suddenly got visited by police officers and carted off to jail because of parking tickets or overdue library books or something unexpected like that.

He laughed. "I'm not sure they'd send a detective for anything like that. You'd probably get a uniformed man or woman."

She laughed. "Then I'm not going to get the chair?"

"I hope not. You're too pretty for that."

She felt her cheeks grow hot with the compliment. After three years with Roger— But she stopped herself. She was training her mind to change the subject whenever the name Roger appeared on the screen in her mind. It was over now. She'd learned many bitter lessons and there was no sense dwelling on failure.

"Thank you."

"My pleasure."

Then Detective Gage leaned forward and dropped a small black notebook on her desk.

"We found this on a man last night."

"He's dead?"

"Yes," Detective Gage said. "Murdered."

Now as much as she felt fear, Meredith felt curiosity. Why would a detective come here to tell her about a murder? If the victim had been one of her friends—God, she hated even to think of something like that.

"Do you know a man named Myles?"

23

"I don't think so."

"Jacob Myles."

She started to say no again and then stopped. Myles. Jacob Myles. The name had a vague ring to it. But why?

Gage watched her intently. "Are you changing your mind?"

"Can you tell me anything about him?"

"Not much except that he lived in a small apartment in Evanston, was unmarried, had a Pekinese dog, and was considered very odd by the other people in the apartment house. We also found some things in his apartment that showed he made a point of keeping up on the whereabouts of a certain group of people, including you. Occasionally he'd spend money on an investigative agency tracking them down. Which was odd, given the fact that he didn't seem to have much to spend."

"How old was he?"

"Sixty-six."

"Jacob Myles," she said again. "I'm afraid I—" And then she remembered.

Mr Myles. High school. My God. "What was his occupation?"

"He was a retired teacher."

"Then I did know him. At least I think I did. If he's the man I'm thinking of, he taught me in high school."

"Did you go to school in Chicago?"

She was careful not to answer the question directly. "I went to private school."

He obviously caught her evasion. "Have you heard from Jacob Myles recently?"

"Lord, no. Not in twenty years or more." She leaned forward and put her elbows on her desk. "Why would you come to see me about Mr Myles's death?"

Gage nodded to the black notebook in the evidence bag. "Your name is on the first page of the notebook, along with a note that he was to meet you at nine last night."

"He didn't, if that's what you're asking."

"He didn't contact you in any way?"

"No."

Gage sat back in his chair. From inside his respectable tweed sport jacket he took a small briar pipe. "Trying to quit cigarettes.

24

This is my pacifier."

"I love the smell of pipes, actually."

"Good." He smiled. "Got any tobacco so I can fill up and have a smoke?"

She liked his sense of humour. "I don't want to be charged with contributing to the delinquency of a detective." Her eyes narrowed again. She was still bothered by her name appearing in Mr Myles's notebook. "Why would he want to contact me after all these years?"

"I was hoping you could tell me."

She shook her head. "I'm afraid I can't. I don't have a clue."

Gage was about to say something, but her intercom buzzed. "Yes?" she said.

"Wondered if you could take lunch a little early today?" Todd said.

"Sure."

"I'd appreciate it. My lunch date just phoned and said she had to go early so—"

"No problem. I'll leave in a few minutes."

"Thanks."

Now Gage said, "Good places to eat around here?"

"Not bad."

"Meeting your husband or anybody?"

She laughed. "I saw you looking for a wedding ring. Believe me, if I were married I'd be wearing one."

"I'm sure you would." He smiled at her but, curiously, the shadow of sorrow was in his gaze again. "Generally I can size up people well. You look like a woman of principle to me and I admire that."

"Will you tell me some war stories?"

"Huh?"

"Well, the least I should get from lunch with a cop is some good war stories. You know, how you single-handedly stopped corruption in the Richie Daley administration."

He grinned. "I'm afraid that would take more than one man. More like an army."

She stood up, feeling almost ridiculously happy. She hadn't had even the merest kind of date in the five months since she'd finally left Roger. She was looking forward to this. Gage seemed to be as lonely as she was.

In the elevator she said, "I didn't notice a wedding ring on your finger either."

He glanced at her. No smile this time. Quite seriously, he said, "That's where we're different."

"Oh?"

"Yes," he said. "I, unfortunately, am married."

Neither of them said another word until they were out of the building and caught up in the lunchtime crowds teeming down North Michigan Avenue this fine fall afternoon.

II

HENRY CROFT tried never to say or even think the word. It was difficult, especially on the days when he needed to get groceries and had to walk three long blocks to the supermarket.

Croft was a sixty-six-year-old retired professor who was living out his days in a messy but decent apartment located between the white bastion of Chicago's North Side and the black bastion of the South Side.

His particular neighbourhood was getting more and more black and they did not seem to be the kind of people, the teenagers especially, who much liked white folks.

Making his way to the supermarket on this sunny morning, dressed in his usual bow tie and rumpled suit, Croft hoped the teenagers wouldn't be on the corner today. He feared them, sure, but even more he disliked their taunts. All his life he'd been bookish and odd. He didn't need any more reminders of that, especially from spiteful young hoodlums.

Croft passed by a variety of shops. Artisans had found this area a good place to be because of low rents and relatively easy parking. It seemed half the antique dealers in the city had decided to relocate here.

Behind him now, Croft heard the familiar rumble of the El, the city's famous overhead railroad. When he'd first moved here thirty years ago, he'd spent many idle hours sitting on the El and touring the city. These days, of course, the El was no longer as safe. A person would be asking for it to spend a day on the El.

The teenagers were on the corner.

Croft saw them from half a block away and his stomach tightened. A part of him wanted to flee and run. Another part of him wanted to buy a gun and start shooting.

He hesitated momentarily, looking back over his shoulder.

He could take the long way around and come into the supermarket from the south instead of the north, bypassing the teenagers entirely.

And then, as he looked at their faces, the word came to mind that Croft hated so much: niggers.

Ever since serving in an integrated unit in World War II, Croft had supported civil rights. He'd even gone to Selma, Alabama, to march with Martin Luther King.

But living in this neighbourhood the past five years had brought back some of the prejudices his white middle-class parents had taught him as a boy—blacks were lazy... blacks were thieves... blacks were violent. He had seen evidence of all these things in this neighbourhood. And no matter how hard he tried not to say or even think the word, it sometimes came to mind.

As now.

He put his head down and marched forward. He had as much right to this street as they did. He would not let them intimidate him, no matter what they said or did. He was an old man and he deserved the dignity of being left alone.

He passed by walls covered with graffiti, by storefronts covered with metal caging to keep out vandals, and finally he came to the corner with the punks.

There were four of them and they looked to be high school age. But, of course, they weren't in class; they were out on the street.

One of them, wearing a yellow bandanna on his head, whistled. "Now that old man walks real sweet, don't he, bro?"

And the others giggled.

Croft kept going.

"Hey, I like that shoppin' bag he carries, man," another of

27

the punks laughed. "My granma got one jus' like it."

"He *is* your granma, man," the third one laughed.

Croft was abreast of them now and he stared directly at their black faces so filled with ignorance and pain and hatred of him, even though he'd done nothing to them. If they hadn't humiliated him every time, perhaps he could feel more sympathy for them, but over the past several months they had said so many degrading things to him that he no longer cared about the conditions that had turned them into such animals.

He just wanted to get to the store.

On his way back he would take the long way around.

He was tired of them and tired of their taunts.

He was one step past them when one of the boys broke from the protection of the pack and pushed him.

Croft stuck his arms out to retain his balance, but the push had surprised him too much. He stumbled right to the edge of the kerb and sprawled facedown into the street.

For the next minute or so, as the boys stood over him and laughed, Croft was treated to a view of the gutter, to viscous patches of motor oil, to sand, to cigarette butts, and even to a used condom somebody had probably tossed from a parked car.

Not one of the boys leaned down to help him up.

"His nice little bow tie got all dirty," a boy said, and giggled.

"Yeah, man, that's one bad tie all right."

"Like to have me one jus' like it."

Croft put his palms flat against the sandy gutter and began the arduous process of regaining his feet.

He no longer heard their jibes because he was making plans for what he'd do once he was upright again and facing them.

He knew there was some risk involved in what he was considering, but at this point he was too angry to care. Maybe he wouldn't be able to do it. At Perpetual Light they'd discovered that powers diminished with age. By the time you were in your forties, your powers were only half what they'd been. But they'd also discovered that moments of acute stress sometimes brought the powers back. And this was certainly a moment of acute stress...

He got to his feet, brushed himself off, and quickly selected the one he wanted, the tallest of them.

He stared directly at the kid and then did it.

Croft's first thought was that he'd failed. The kid didn't react at all.

One or two of the other kids were taunting Croft again, but Croft paid no attention. He just desperately kept staring at the tall boy.

And then the boy jumped, the way Croft had seen others jump when it happened.

"Hey!" the boy said, grasping both sides of his head. "Hey! What're you doin', man?"

His friends thought the boy was kidding. They slapped at him and laughed and did imitations of him using his hands as a vice.

They didn't even notice when Croft slipped away and moved on down the street to the supermarket.

By now the tall boy was in the middle of the sidewalk, flat on his back, and turning in crazed circles like an animal that had been badly injured and was caught up in panic. At least his friends no longer deluded themselves that this was some kind of joke. They looked scared.

Croft always got the same items, rye bread and Philadelphia cream cheese and skim milk and dill pickles and green peppers and luncheon meat and a frozen Sara Lee chocolate cake. Oh, yes, and a six-pack of ginger ale for when he sat up late and watched old movies on cable.

He took the southern route back, not because he was afraid but because he wanted to enjoy the day. Even in the city, autumn's aromas were pleasant, and the slant of thinning fall sunlight was beautiful on the brilliant leaves.

He was a block from his apartment when it happened.

He was practised enough at receiving that he didn't jerk about, as the black kid had done, he simply stopped walking and opened his mind.

He wasn't frightened, but he was curious.

29

The signal was incredibly powerful. He thought of all the days at Perpetual Light. Testing the best of them. How powerful their signals had been...

And then it was gone. Like that. So quickly come and gone that Croft wondered if the experience hadn't been illusory in some way. They'd always talked about residual contacts, not unlike the 'flashbacks' LSD users reported—the mind re-creating the entire experience for reasons nobody could ever determine. Maybe Croft had just had a flashback, a tribute to the days when he'd been intensely pursuing the whole matter.

He began walking again.

What the hell had just happened?

Even if it wasn't a flashback, even if it was the real thing, who could possibly have sent a signal that powerful?

His entire mind had been rocked for a moment there.

He started walking faster now. He wanted to be in his apartment, the door locked.

Suddenly, he was afraid, far more afraid than the corner boys had ever made him.

III

SHE WASN'T exactly lying to him, but Gage knew that she was keeping something back.

They ate lunch in a crowded sandwich shop where most of the talk seemed to be about the important Bears game this coming Sunday, and where the waitresses all wore Bear pins on the lapels of their mini-skirted uniforms.

Gage spent extra minutes on the menu because, at thirty-eight, he'd decided it was time to start considering his eating habits. He'd put on ten pounds since he'd quit smoking a year ago and had developed this incredible appetite for sweets.

He ordered a salad and a bowl of tomato soup. Meredith had a salad and two Saltine crackers.

While they ate, Gage kept the conversation light. This was easy to do with a woman as attractive as Meredith Sawyer. She wasn't a glamorous model, but her sweet face and trim body were definitely appealing.

They talked about the magazine, and incidents in Chicago history—he'd always been fascinated by the aftermath of the Haymarket Square Riots and the era of Al Capone in particular. Then they discussed the local political scene, both admitting that they'd shifted from being lifelong Democrats to being Independents who occasionally voted for—unthinkable as it was—Republicans, particularly the Cook County group of Reform Republicans.

Over coffee he brought up the murdered man again, and it was then that it became clear Meredith was keeping something from him.

"So you haven't heard from him in years?"

"Not years. Decades. Literally."

"And he was your teacher in high school?"

"Yes."

"And that was a private school?"

"Yes."

He decided to try his luck again. The first time he'd asked this question, she'd glossed over it. "And this was a school in Chicago?"

She looked at him a long moment, like a quiz show contestant who is not quite sure what to answer. "Near Chicago."

"Oh. Near Chicago." He smiled. He wanted to take some of the sting from his questions. "And I take it that the school had a name?"

"Yes."

He laughed. "You're going to make me get this out of you question by question, aren't you?"

"I'm sorry," she said, and looked suddenly flustered and flushed. "I don't mean to be evasive. I really don't." She straightened up in her chair, as if announcing that she was now going to take a different tack. "The name of the school was the Perpetual Light Institute."

"A religious school?"

"No. Even though it sounds that way, doesn't it?"

He decided to try another approach to find out about her parents and her background. "Must have been expensive."

She hesitated again, choosing her words carefully. "No. Not

31

really."

"And you graduated from there?"

She smiled. It had been a while. "Yes, and believe it or not, with honours."

"I'm proud of you."

"So was I, actually." She lifted her coffee cup and sipped.

"How about right after school? Did Mr Myles keep in touch with you then?"

She shook her head. "No."

"So since graduation you haven't heard anything from him?"

"Not from Mr Myles."

"But from others at the school?"

"From others at the school—yes. For a while I did, anyway." She was being evasive again.

She wasn't good at lying, Gage thought. That's a good sign.

"Do they have reunions?" he asked.

"Not really."

"So you haven't been back there."

"Not in—a while."

"I see."

Her cheeks were flushed again. She looked nervous, uncomfortable. "I'm sorry I'm not being more helpful."

"Oh, you're helping me all right." He laughed. "It's just taking me a little longer than usual."

The waitress came back with their bill. Meredith insisted on going Dutch, even splitting the tip.

My kind of woman, Gage thought ironically, trying not to think of Kathleen and his life with her in the past two years.

Meredith stood up. She was lovely in her tailored grey suit. "I've really got to be getting back."

He put out his hand, careful not to be macho and give her a death-lock grip, but not giving her a wimpy grip either.

"I'm sure I'll be talking with you again, Meredith," he said. He liked saying her name.

Earlier he'd had the impression that she found him interesting if not downright attractive. But now he could see that she'd drawn into herself and just wanted to be away from him.

"That would be nice," she said, glancing at the front door of the sandwich shop.

"I'll walk you back," he said.

"Oh, no. You've got things to do, and walking alone sometimes helps me gather my thoughts. Thanks for a nice lunch."

"My pleasure."

And with that she was gone. Technically, since this was a police interview, he should have been the one who ended the lunch. But he decided that now was no time to pull rank.

She worked her way gracefully through the crowd of people thronged around the cash register, and vanished into the men and women who packed the street outside.

Gage was more curious than ever. Maybe she wasn't simply being evasive after all. Maybe she knew something about Myles's murder and had decided not to co-operate.

IV

WHEN HE GOT HOME, Croft set both deadbolts. He then hurried to the bedroom, where he took a thirty-eight from a bureau drawer.

He returned to the living room of his small, shabby apartment and lifted the receiver on the old black rotary telephone.

This was not a number he needed to look up. Even though he had not called it for many years, he dialled it quickly.

He could hear adjustments being made in the telephone circuitry. This was a ship-to-shore call. Then a male voice came on. It said, "How may I help you?"

"This is Croft. I need to speak to Candelmas."

"I'm afraid that's impossible, sir."

"Croft, Croft. Don't you know who I am?"

"I'm afraid I don't, sir."

"How long have you worked on his yacht?"

"Three years, sir."

"And in all that time he hasn't mentioned me?"

"I'm afraid not, sir."

Croft sighed. His body was cold from icy sweat. Only now was he beginning to understand the full implications of what

33

had happened to him on his way back from the supermarket. "Then give him a message."

"All right, sir."

"Tell him Croft called and I said that somebody's come back. Somebody with remarkable gifts."

"Somebody with remarkable gifts?"

"He'll know what I'm talking about."

"Yes, sir. I'll give him the message."

"And also give him my phone number." Croft repeated it twice.

"Very good, sir."

Croft could imagine how he sounded to the young man on the phone. Crazed, no doubt; a crazed old man.

But that's how Candelmas would sound, too, once he learned what was going on.

Croft went to pour himself a large drink of whiskey.

1

I

A WEEK LATER Meredith endured a blind date. She knew things were going to be bad when he showed up forty-five minutes late and offered neither an explanation nor an apology. He didn't help matters by saying, "But you know how guys are, babe." In the best of circumstances, she didn't like being called 'babe' and these were hardly the best of circumstances.

She had to grant that he was good-looking, as her friend Jane Hirschbaum had promised. But that was about the only thing Kevin Del Ray had going for him. At Morton's, a fine red-meat restaurant near the Newberry Library, he made a very big thing of ordering the wine in French and of winking at the waitress, who did seem to find him awfully cute. Even before dinner he covered Meredith's small hand in his big one, and said, "You may as well get it over with."

"Pardon me?"

"Tell me who I look like."

"Oh? And who would that be?"

He grinned with calculated boyishness. "C'mon, babe, everybody says I look like him. Even guys."

She narrowed her eyes, as if scrutinising him carefully. "Gee," she said. "You've got me."

"Gable."

"Gable?"

"Clark."

She decided to deflate him utterly. He had plenty of egotism to fall back on. It wasn't as if she were going to crush him for life.

"People really think you look like Clark Gable?" she said. "How interesting."

For the next half-hour, he sulked.

His depression seemed to cheer her up. She chattered amiably on about various historical events, including the time in 1932 when Chicago teachers marched in the streets to protest the fact that the school board could not pay them. Many teachers were so dedicated that they worked through the entire Depression without ever once being paid.

Hers were not the type of anecdotes that Kevin found interesting. He was more the dirty-joke type. He moved automatically from sulking into boredom. Now he wanted out of this date as badly as Meredith did. This was right where Meredith wanted him.

Following dinner, he got back on the Dan Ryan and aimed his Datsun Z like an arrow straight for her apartment house.

He sang along with a Billy Joel tape and scarcely said anything to Meredith. She did not feel neglected.

Finally, as he approached her place in the maze of dark streets, he said, "Can I ask you something?"

"Sure."

"You were putting me on, weren't you?"

"Putting you on?"

"You really do think I look like Clark Gable, don't you?"

She weakened. She didn't want to, but she did. This guy had such a delicate ego that she just couldn't do any more of a job on him.

She sighed. "Yes, I guess you do."

"Good. I'm glad you said that."

"Oh? Why?"

"Because otherwise I wouldn't have come up for a drink."

She started to say something really nasty but then stopped herself. Calmly, she said, "I'm afraid I'm getting the flu."

"Really?"

"Umm-hmm. Sore throat. Sick stomach."

She sensed that for all his macho posturing, he was the hypochondriac type. Pretty boys often were.

She watched him angle himself away from her, avoiding her. In profile, the green light of the dashboard played across his features. He really did look like Clark Gable.

They were half a block from her house when she felt it. No doubt what it was.

She writhed in her seat and began gasping.

"Hey," he said, startled. "Are you all right?"

She was shaky. "I just need to get home."

"You're not—nauseous, are you? No offence, but these are real leather seats."

"Just—hurry."

He floored the Z.

He pulled into her parking lot doing fifty miles per hour, slammed the brakes on when he came even with her door, and said, "You want me to walk you upstairs?" Meaning, of course, that he didn't want to.

She wanted to say, *Clark Gable would have walked me up the stairs*, but she was too frightened right now for jokes.

She got out of the car.

Inevitably, just as her door was closing, he leaned forward and said, "Ciao, babe."

She watched him whip a U-turn and roar out of the parking lot. He left her to the silence of an unseasonably warm autumn night, one brilliant with stars and the smoky scents of the season.

She knew what had happened to her. She just couldn't believe it. After all these years…

She turned around and faced the steps leading to her section of the apartment house. She took hold of the black iron railing and made her way upward, feeling like a doddering old lady.

Nothing else happened the rest of the night, but despite a Xanax and a glass of warm milk, she did not sleep till nearly dawn.

II

"SAY, THAT DATE of yours must have worked out pretty well last night, eh?" Todd Benjamin said when she walked into the magazine office next morning.

"I look tired, huh?"

"No offence but you look exhausted." He grinned. "He must have been a winner."

She smiled demurely. "Oh, yes," she said, "He looked just like Clark Gable."

She snatched a cup of coffee from Mr Coffee and then went to her desk and got to work.

During WWII the 'sin' district of New Orleans, then known as Storyville, was closed down, and many, if not most, jazz musicians were forced to leave their beloved city. The majority of them headed to Chicago, which was how the city came to be the centre of jazz, when musicians such as Louis Armstrong found a natural home in the speakeasies and night-clubs of the era. The gangsters of the time were especially supportive. Though their ethnic roots were very different from those of black musicians, the gangsters took to jazz with a ferocious and possessive love, club owners paying big and competitive dollars to steal musicians away from each other.

Around ten, Meredith took a break from her morning's work and went to stand by her window, looking down on Michigan Avenue, sparkling in the autumn sunshine. Several times this morning she'd started wondering again why she hadn't heard from Detective Gage. Not only was she curious about the progress of the murder case, she was also curious about Gage himself. What had he meant exactly when he said that he was married, "unfortunately." Had he meant that he found marriage too confining or had he meant something else?

Then she thought of the incident in the car last night. She

didn't wonder at all what had taken place. She knew exactly. It was just that it had been so many years since… since somebody had been monitoring her.

She was about to return to the typewriter when her phone rang. She leaned over the desk and picked it up.

"Hello."

An old woman's voice said, "Meredith?"

"Yes."

Pause. "You probably don't remember me." Pause. "Mrs Frommer."

Mrs Frommer? "The name is familiar, Mrs Frommer, but—"

"Perpetual Light."

"Oh, why, yes."

"I was one of the housekeepers."

"Of course." By now Meredith's voice had warmed considerably. Not only did she recall the woman, she recalled her fondly. Mrs Frommer was one of those sturdy, reliable, and necessary women in a private school. She'd taken a special interest in Meredith and always had an apple or a piece of candy, or just a tender smile for the girl. "This is really a surprise."

"It's been many years. It took me a while to track you down but you were always so friendly I didn't think you'd mind and—"

"How have you been, Mrs Frommer?" My Lord, Meredith thought, the woman must be in her seventies by now.

"Oh—good." The woman sounded hesitant again. Then, "Do you know where Wrigleyville is?"

"Of course."

"I live near there. I was wondering if you could—come see me tonight."

At least I don't have to worry about my social calendar conflicting with anything, Meredith thought, smiling to herself. Tonight was just going to be an evening of air-popped popcorn and sit-coms anyway. "I'd love to see you."

"Good. Here's my address."

Meredith wrote it down and then said, "Mrs Frommer?"

"Yes."

"Is—everything all right?"

Pause. "I'm not sure, Meredith. That's why I want to talk to you."

"I look forward to seeing you again." And she did. Meredith had many memories of Perpetual Light, and Mrs Frommer was among the best of them.

"I'll see you tonight," Mrs Frommer said. And then, "You've always been such a good girl, Meredith. You really have." And then she hung up.

Not until an hour later, when Meredith was finishing up her story on the origins of Chicago jazz, did the extraordinary events of the past week strike her. First the murder of one of her former teachers, a man who died with Meredith's name written in his notebook; and now, after nearly two decades, an unexpected call from Mrs Frommer.

What was going on here?

Why was she being drawn inexorably back to Perpetual Light?

III

HIS WIFE SAID, "You know I'm in love with another man, Gage. Can't you make it easy for everybody involved?"

She'd always called him Gage, ever since they'd gone to Loyola together back in the waning days of the Vietnam War.

The marriage counsellor wore a blue turtleneck sweater, designer jeans and cordovan penny loafers without socks. He was tall and muscular in the way of a pro basketball player, and he combed his greying brown hair in such a way that he only drew attention to his baldness. His name was Cotter and he'd been recommended by a detective Gage knew at the Sixth Precinct. Cotter had saved the detective's marriage. He didn't seem to be having the same kind of luck with Gage and his wife.

Kathleen glanced at her watch. "I'm sorry, Gage, but I've really got to be getting back to work."

Gage looked over at Cotter, as if Cotter might have some sort of answer for this dilemma. Kathleen hadn't wanted to

39

come to a marriage counsellor in the first place. According to her, the marriage was finished and there was nothing to discuss. But Gage had persisted and so she'd reluctantly agreed to three sessions. This was the third.

Cotter said, "You must have a very demanding boss, Kathleen. Not even letting you take a full hour for a counselling session."

Kathleen, a beautiful brunette whose very haughtiness was a big part of her appeal, shook her head. "I know I come off like a real bitch in these sessions. And I'm sorry. For everybody's sake. It's just—" She glanced at Gage and frowned. "I wish our marriage had worked out better, Gage. I wish I'd been the woman you thought I was, and I wish you'd been the man I thought you were. But we let each other down. As far as I'm concerned, nobody's right and nobody's wrong. I happened to fall in love with somebody else because I wasn't getting what I needed from our marriage. I didn't do it on purpose and I didn't do it to hurt you. I—just fell in love is all. And now I want to marry this man." Now she looked at Cotter. "In order to do that, I need a divorce. That's what I can't make Gage understand. That there's no point in spending any more time or money in trying to patch up our marriage. It's over. And we may as well get on with the divorce."

She checked her watch again. She looked especially fetching today in her black sweater and tan suede skirt. "I really have to be going," she said, and stood up.

It was not a dramatic moment—no shouting, no tears, nothing being smashed—but Gage recognised it for exactly what it was. Their final moment as husband and wife. From now on there would be just the lawyers and the divorce papers and the final resolution with an overworked judge somewhere.

She nodded good-bye to them and then looked softly at Gage. "Take care of yourself, Gage." There was a catch in her throat that Gage knew to be genuine.

She walked across the small room that was filled with sombre bookcases and well-tended hanging plants. She closed the door gently behind her.

The two men sat in silence. Gage sensed that he was in shock. His marriage was definitely over. No amount of loving her, no

40

amount of trying to make things right again, would work.

"I have a pint of bourbon in my desk," Cotter said after a time.

"No, thanks."

"I can imagine how rough that was on you."

Gage looked at him. "I wish I could hate her. I wish I could blame her. The hell of it is, she's right. We weren't very good marriage partners."

Cotter smiled sadly. "That's the beginning of wisdom, my friend."

"I wish I were pissed off. It'd make this moment a lot easier for me."

"Yes, it probably would."

Gage sighed. " Nearly fourteen years."

"No children, though, Gage. Fortunately."

"They were going to come along, kids. But somehow they never did." For the first time, bitterness sounded in his voice. "Along with a lot of other things that never materialised, I guess."

"Got any plans for tonight?"

"I'm doubling up. Working two shifts. My partner's taking a week off."

"Good. I was going to suggest that you keep yourself occupied."

Gage nodded. "I'm going to have to do that a lot, aren't I? Keep myself occupied?"

"Anybody you've thought about dating?"

"Not really." Then he thought of Meredith. Despite her aversion to answering his questions, she'd struck him as an intelligent and attractive woman. "Well, one I guess, but it would be sort of a hassle."

"Oh?"

"Yes, she's involved in a homicide case I'm working on."

"As a suspect?"

"No." Gage laughed. "Nothing that romantic. But she did know the victim and for some reason she doesn't want to talk about it."

"But you want to see her anyway?"

"Yes. She seems—nice. Gentle. Sweet in a modern sort of

41

way." Gage looked at the door his wife had just walked out of… "That's one thing Kathleen never was, I guess."

"Sweet?"

"Right. Not much of a friend when you came down to it. When she got in bad moods, she didn't want to talk to anybody, including me. And when I had problems—well, she thought I should keep them to myself too."

"A lot of people are like that."

Gage nodded. "I guess. I just don't want to be one of them."

Gage glanced at his watch. "Well," he said, putting his palms on his knees and starting to push himself to his feet.

"You've had a big day."

"I have at that, haven't I?"

"You're strong enough to handle this, Gage, and you know it."

"I'm just going to be lonely for a while."

"No more lonely than you've been the last few years with Kathleen."

Gage grinned sadly. "That's sure the truth, now, isn't it?"

In five minutes he was down in the parking lot, pulling his conservative blue Buick into the street.

IV

PINK PHONE MESSAGES littered his desk. Gage made two stacks of them, urgent and not urgent. One of the urgent ones belonged to a man named Chesmore. His name had also been written in Jacob Myles's small black notebook, along with a phone number and a recent date. Gage had called Chesmore several times, and had stopped by his house several times in the past week, too. There had been no response whatsoever. He had begun to think that Chesmore might be on vacation. Now Chesmore was calling him. Curious.

He dialled the number.

"Hello," said an older woman's voice.

"This is Detective Gage. I'm calling for Mr Chesmore."

"Oh, Detective Gage. I'm his sister, Mrs Kubicek. I'm the one who called you."

"Oh?"

"Yes, I was just pulling up the other day when I saw you leaving. The neighbours said you'd stopped several times and asked about George and you left a card saying you were a policeman. I understand you wanted to talk to George."

"Yes, that's right."

"Well, George isn't there."

"So I gathered. Is he on vacation?"

"No, not vacation." She hesitated. "He's in the hospital."

"Did he have a stroke or something?"

"Not that kind of hospital. A mental hospital."

"I see. This is a recent development?"

"Four nights ago. He called me and told me he was feeling very strange and that he was afraid of what he might do to himself. He's taken medicine for years. He suffers from depression. Manic depression is the proper term, I guess."

"I see."

"So anyway I told him I'd come over and spend the night with him—he's lived alone since his wife died eight years ago and my husband doesn't mind when I spend an occasional night over to my brother's—but George said no. He said it was more serious than that. He said if he got in the mood to injure himself, I wouldn't be able to stop him. He was real scared. I'd never heard him like that before."

"So what happened?"

"He asked me to call St. Michael's."

"And you took him there?"

"Yes. The doctors tell me they're considering giving him those—oh, you know—electrical—"

"Electroshock therapy."

"That's it."

This was probably all coincidental, but still Gage considered it curious. Plus it gave him something to do other than feel sorry for himself. "Can your brother have visitors, Mrs Kubicek?"

"I think so."

"Good. Oh. Did he know a man named Jacob Myles?"

"Myles... Myles. Gosh, to be honest, I just don't know."

"Thanks, Mrs Kubicek."

"Say, I never did ask you."

"Ask me?"

"George. He isn't in any trouble or anything, is he?"

"No, Mrs Kubicek. I just had some questions for him."

"I see. Well, good luck, Detective."

"Thanks, again."

1

I

AFTER WORK Meredith took the Dan Ryan home, did twenty minutes of exercises along with two women on cable TV, showered, and then fixed herself a dinner of sliced turkey breast, spinach, and a piece of wheat toast. Once or twice a week she splurged and stopped at Baskin-Robbins for a sundae. Women do not live by sensible diets alone.

She was closing the drapes of her apartment when she looked down at the empty lot and saw the blonde woman in the dark glasses and green headscarf behind the wheel of a grey Volvo sedan. The woman appeared to be looking directly up at Meredith's apartment.

Meredith wasn't certain why, but she shuddered.

There was something familiar and unnerving about the woman. She pulled the drapes closed. If the woman was waiting for Meredith to come down to the north lot, she would be disappointed. Meredith always parked in the south lot.

She closed the door behind her and went down the stairs. Once she was in her car, she decided to drive to the north lot for a closer look at the woman.

When she got there, the grey Volvo was gone, as was the woman.

Meredith smiled at herself. Sometimes she got idiotically paranoid. The fortunes, she supposed, of living in big-city America near the end of this century.

HE HEARD CRIES. They were more violent than sad, and for a moment he wondered whom they belonged to, what kind of mental torture had brought him to this place. God knew, Gage was familiar with mental torture. That was a perfect description of the last years of his marriage.

He went into the white lobby and up to the reception desk. The cries from upstairs had faded now. No doubt the man had become violent and no doubt someone had given him a few cc's of something appropriate to calm him down.

"May I help you?"

Gage showed his badge. "I'd like to speak with Mr Chesmore if that's possible."

The nurse quickly consulted her list of patients. "You'd have to speak with Dr Birnbaum. He's making his rounds right now. If you'd like to take a seat over there, I'll be happy to send him over when he gets back down here."

Gage nodded his thanks and found a seat for himself. The reading material ran to year-old issues of Time magazine and the usual battered copies of hunting and fishing journals. Gage wasn't much of an outdoorsman. He preferred an invigorating night of watching a good Bogart movie on the tube.

Dr Birnbaum, a tall and sombre man in a white medical smock, appeared in fifteen minutes.

"You're Detective Gage?" he said, putting out a slender but powerful hand. "Nice to meet you. I understand you'd like to see Mr Chesmore."

"Yes, I would."

"Is it very important?"

"It could be. I'm working on a homicide case."

"I see. Hmm." Dr Birnbaum seemed to carry on a silent conversation with himself, debating what to say next. "Are you aware of why he's here?"

"No, I'm not, Doctor."

"Shock."

"I see."

"So far he's eluded all our tests. We can't explain it." He smiled. "Isn't that a terrible thing for an arrogant medical man with millions of dollars of equipment at his disposal to admit? That we can't explain it?"

"Is he violent?" Gage asked, thinking about the cries he'd heard when he first entered the hospital.

"Quite the contrary. We could barely get a pulse when he came in here. His vital signs still haven't improved all that much."

"And you're not making any guesses at what caused it?"

Dr Birnbaum shrugged. "There's no intelligent guess to make. A neurologist spent half the afternoon with Chesmore. He doesn't have a clue either."

"So what happens to him?"

"Well, I suppose we must assume that his present state is the result of an injury of some kind. The neurologist has eliminated tumour but he hasn't eliminated trauma."

"Meaning?"

"Meaning, Mr Chesmore may have fallen and done considerable damage to himself in some way we can't detect as yet."

"So for now he stays in his hospital bed?"

"Right."

Gage dug out a small business card and handed it to the doctor. "I'd appreciate you letting me know when I can see him."

"Of course, of course."

"Thanks for your time."

"My pleasure." Dr Birnbaum turned and walked back toward the elevators.

On the way out the front door, Gage heard the cries again. So lonely, so sad, those cries.

Even when he got to his car and turned up a Bruce Springsteen tape, he could hear the cries of that poor caged man. He turned Springsteen up even louder.

III

WRIGLEYVILLE was changing. Until a few years ago the neighbourhood had been almost quaintly blue collar, not having

46

evolved much from the thirties. The big draw had always been Wrigley Field, of course, home of the Cubs. But over the past five years, parts of the area had taken on a different look where the punk and gay cultures displayed themselves.

As she drove the dark streets Meredith kept thinking about the curious woman in her parking lot. Why had she looked familiar? And what had she been doing out there? Even though the woman had been gone by the time Meredith reached that section of the lot, she was still troubled by her presence.

Mrs Frommer lived in the oldest section of Wrigleyville, on a short block that looked as if the same aluminium-siding salesman had signed everybody up at the same time. The cars parked on the street were not new, but they had been well taken care of. There was the obstinate pride of hard work apparent in everything about this neighbourhood, and Meredith was impressed with how well the people here took care of themselves.

She parked and got out. Wind skittered fallen leaves along the sidewalk. They made a brittle sound, skeleton fingers on a graveyard headstone, which was an image from a horror story she'd read as a girl.

She passed four houses before coming to the right one.

No lights shone in Mrs Frommer's place. Curious.

Meredith went up to the gate, unlatched it, and went inside the yard. Mrs Frommer's place was a one-storey house with a big statue of the Virgin standing near the stairs and a screened-in porch running the length of the front. No sound came from inside. Somewhere nearby a dog yipped and a train rushed through the night. The wind whined in the trees now.

Meredith felt uncomfortable being here. They'd had an appointment. Lights should be on.

She passed the statue of the Virgin, noticing how crudely the face had been sculpted, and went up the three steps to the porch.

She knocked loudly and waited. No response came. She tried again. Once more, no response.

A light went on inside.

A small, stocky woman appeared and came to open the porch

door for Meredith.

"I just wanted to be sure it was you, Meredith," the woman said.

She turned around and led them back inside.

The smells struck Meredith first, years of smells lying on the air of this small, venerable house—cabbage and incense, brownies and furniture polish, and dozens more. They were familiar and pleasant smells individually, but collectively they were almost oppressive.

The living room looked as if it had been intentionally preserved this way since 1948. The horsehair couch was covered with huge antimacassars. The linen lampshade seemed to smother the light, casting the room into long, grave shadows. A carefully polished console radio stood in one corner, playing Czech music at a low volume. There was no evidence of TV. The hardwood floors were covered by wool throw rugs, darkly dyed. And Mrs Frommer complemented this room perfectly. In her flowered housedress, durable brown oxfords, and crudely cut grey hair, she looked like an ethnic visitor who had just stepped from a time warp.

Meredith recognised the woman immediately.

"Stand over by the light," Mrs Frommer said from the shadows. "Let me look at you."

Self-consciously, Meredith stepped into the glow cast by the lamp.

Mrs Frommer smiled. "You've become a beautiful young woman."

Meredith laughed. "Beautiful is overdoing it a little, Mrs Frommer."

"Beautiful to me, anyway," Mrs Frommer said. "But then I was always proud of you. You were my special friend."

Seeing the woman after all these years, Meredith felt the special friendship Mrs Frommer referred to. Meredith had always preferred her to the regular staff. Mrs Frommer had simply been warmer and more giving of herself. She had even shared Meredith's passion for Nancy Drew mysteries.

Thinking of these things, Meredith reached out her arms and took Mrs Frommer to her. The woman hugged her back.

They stood for a long moment embracing. Mrs Frommer felt as solid and reliable as ever. Age had not made her fragile. Meredith was happy to know this.

"You'd like some coffee, I'll bet."

"That would be nice, but only if it's no trouble."

Mrs Frommer smiled. "No. Just like the old days, Meredith, I keep a pot going all the time. I know they say it's bad for you but it doesn't seem to have hurt me any and I'm seventy-five years old." She mentioned this last fact with obvious pride. Looking at the woman, Meredith couldn't believe it—so spry... so filled with life... seventy-five years old... impossible to believe.

When Mrs Frommer left the living room, Meredith seated herself carefully on the horsehair couch. Like the rest of the furnishings, this was beautifully preserved, almost as if nobody had ever sat on it.

She wondered why Mrs Frommer had called her. Had the woman simply got sentimental? Somehow, Meredith doubted it.

Mrs Frommer was back in less than two minutes, carrying a sterling silver tray. Two cups of coffee in delicate china cups rode the centre of the tray. Festive cookies sat in the centre of a matching saucer.

Meredith laughed. "I see you remembered my sweet tooth."

"Oh, I remember more than that, Meredith," the woman said. There was no humour in her tone.

Mrs Frommer seated herself in a deep armchair. In the shadows of the room, she looked old and weary for the first time. She sipped coffee and munched on the corners of her cookie, but her eyes never left Meredith's face.

"You remember Dr Candelmas, no doubt?"

Meredith tried to lighten the mood. "Who could forget Dr Candelmas? The original bogeyman himself."

"Do you ever hear from him?"

"Good heavens, no. Do you?"

Mrs Frommer shook her head. "Not in twenty years." Finished with her cookie, she picked up her coffee again. Sipped. "I wondered if you would help me locate Dr Candelmas."

Meredith said, "Why would you want to contact him after all these years?"

"Reasons of my own." She smiled. "I don't mean to be mysterious, Meredith, it's just that lately— Well, there are some things I'd like to discuss with him. I just thought—Well, you were always one of his favourites."

Meredith shook her head. "My sister was one of his favourites, Mrs Frommer. He liked me well enough, I suppose, but it was Valerie he really adored."

The woman's gaze dropped momentarily. "I'm sorry about what happened to her, Meredith. I know what a shock that was to you."

Meredith nodded. "I'll always remember it. The worst of the pain is gone now, but I still think about it at least once or twice a day." She frowned. "I suppose it's my morbid side."

"No, not at all. I lost a sister, too—diphtheria. I come from a big family. Eleven kids. But my youngest sister was my favourite. And when she died— Well, I think of her at least once a day, too. I still remember the look on the doctor's face when he came out of Corrine's room. My mother knew what his look meant, too. She just burst into tears. My father had to help her into their bedroom and help her lie down. She just went completely to pieces. I remember that so vividly…" She sighed and brought her gaze back from yesterday. "So I don't think you're being morbid about Valerie at all. You loved her. Her memory should stay fresh with you."

Meredith noticed that Mrs Frommer had become agitated since starting the conversation. She wrung her hands and her neck had seemed to develop a small tic. Meredith thought of the lights being off in the house when she'd first come up. And why, after all these years, would Mrs Frommer want to see Dr Candelmas? He was one person Meredith never wanted to see again.

"The last I heard he was somewhere in the Chicago area," Meredith said.

Mrs Frommer's neck twitched a few more times and then she raised her eyes to Meredith. "Have you been out there lately, Meredith?"

"To Perpetual Light?"

"Yes."

"Not since the day I left. And I don't have any plans to return, either, believe me."

"It burned down."

"So I heard."

Mrs Frommer looked down at her hands in her lap and then up at Meredith. "I drove out there last week."

"But why?"

"Because lately, in my head, I've felt—" She tapped her right temple and then said, "I'm almost afraid to talk."

"How did the place look?" Meredith said. Certain memories of it came to her and she shivered. She tried never to think of Perpetual Light or Dr Candelmas.

"You wouldn't recognise it now," Mrs Frommer said. "The big stone main house is nothing more than a burned-out shell and weeds have grown over everything. It looked pretty sad."

Meredith decided to say it. She felt her friendship with Mrs Frommer was good enough to support a minor inquiry. "Mrs Frommer?"

"Yes?"

"Mrs Frommer, are you all right?"

"I'm not sure what you mean."

"You seem very nervous. And that makes me feel sorry for you."

"I'd just like to see Dr Candelmas is all."

"That's the part I particularly don't understand. Maybe I'm not remembering things properly, but I seem to remember you trying to keep me away from him as much as possible."

Mrs Frommer sighed. "Yes. Yes, I did do that, didn't I?"

"I always had the sense that you were trying to protect me from something."

Mrs Frommer smiled. "I suppose I was, yes."

"And that's what I'm trying to do with you now, Mrs Frommer. Protect you. Whatever's wrong, there's got to be a better solution than looking for Dr Candelmas."

Meredith set down her cup. She needed to go to the bathroom. She was not noted for having a kidney that tolerated much

51

coffee. "May I use your bathroom?"

But Mrs Frommer's attention had drifted off. Only when Meredith quietly repeated the question did the other woman look up. "Of course, of course. Down the hall there and to your right."

On her way to the bathroom, Meredith glanced over many nice antiques, including a genuine loom. In the shadows, the house was pleasantly drafty.

Mrs Frommer had nuked the bathroom with scented aerosol spray. She was of a generation that believed all natural odours were crimes against humanity.

It was chilly in the small bathroom. Not only had Mrs Frommer bombed the room with aerosol, she'd left the frosted window tip several inches to further rid the bathroom of smells.

Meredith was washing her hands when she heard the scream and first smelled the smoke.

Without even drying her hands, she wheeled around in the tiny bathroom and grabbed the doorknob. The door was either locked or stuck.

"Mrs Frommer! Mrs Frommer!"

But Mrs Frommer wasn't listening. She was still screaming. And running around wildly in the living room. Meredith could hear the older woman tipping over furniture and bumping into tables and chairs.

"Mrs Frommer! Mrs Frommer!"

Meredith yanked on the doorknob until her arms hurt, then she placed her bottom against the edge of the sink for leverage and tried to kick the door open. It didn't work.

By now grey, greasy smoke was rolling into the bathroom. Meredith began coughing.

She gave up on the door and turned back to the window, assuming she wouldn't have any trouble pushing it up farther. But Mrs Frommer had shoved the window as far up as it would go. Paint dried long ago kept it from going up even another inch.

Meredith knew she needed to escape the bathroom soon. Even with the window open the thick smoke would soon knock her unconscious. And then...

She lifted the small metal wastecan and smashed out the frosted windowpanes. She then lowered the window frame, took a metal nail file she'd found in the medicine cabinet, and began cutting through the screening.

In all, it took her seven minutes to wriggle her way through the window and drop to the ground below. By the time she'd reached the winter-brown grass, she felt dizzy from inhaling so much smoke, and still frantic about Mrs Frommer.

She took a moment to stand back from the small house. The entire place was in flames. Distantly, she heard the sirens of fire engines.

She ran around to the front of the house and saw that maybe a dozen people had already gathered to watch the blaze that was now lighting up the entire night, lending the darkness an eerie daylight. Faces glowed in the leaping light of the flames.

"My God!" a plump woman wrapped tight in a shabby winter coat said. "I could hear Mrs Frommer screaming!"

By now the fire trucks were closer. Meredith could feel them rumbling down the narrow brick streets.

"No way she could've gotten out of there alive," the plump woman's husband said mournfully. He kept shaking his bald head from side to side.

Meredith just stood there, looking at the flames lapping at the night sky. It was so hot. It must be a hundred degrees or more on the sidewalk here.

Every few minutes a part of the fiery roof would collapse onto the floor below.

Somewhere in there were the remains of Mrs Frommer.

Meredith did her best not to cry—she wanted to be composed when the fire investigators began asking her questions—but finally she could hold her tears no longer.

She thought of Mrs Frommer—and the woman's horrible cries for help—and wept.

4

I

THE YACHT floated on Lake Michigan beneath a full moon. The water sparkled like black diamonds. No other craft could be seen for miles.

Of the crew, only the captain was still awake. He stood at the helm, long hands on the wheel.

In the stillness, black water tapping the sides of the yacht, he heard the cabin door open and Candelmas put in his appearance for the evening.

It was the same each night. The vast fat man in the black silk pyjamas and black silk robe strolled the deck alone, taking huge drags on a long Havana cigar. In the moonlight his thinning white hair seemed to glow.

Candelmas always made three complete turns around the deck, never more, never less. He never acknowledged the captain in any way.

When his third turn was done, Candelmas always walked aft and stood looking out at the endless black night. There was an air of great, almost ponderous sorrow about him. The captain always wondered what could cause a man to exude such grief. But the captain knew better than to ask. He was paid four times more than his last job on a cruise ship, and Candelmas was most generous with Christmas bonuses.

Tonight, Candelmas took something from his robe and held it up to the moonlight.

The captain recognised it immediately as a small, framed photograph. Candelmas's wide shoulders slumped in a sigh that the captain could clearly hear even up here.

Candelmas stood in this way, staring at the photograph, for the next five minutes. He seemed to be mesmerised by it.

After a time, Candelmas slipped the photograph back in the pocket of his black silk robe and shook his head. Again, the impression the captain got was of deep sorrow.

Candelmas turned around and walked back to the cabin and disappeared quickly downstairs. He moved quite gracefully for a man of his bulk.

The captain returned his attention to the yacht. He liked late nights alone up here. A philosophical man, he liked to look up at the stars and then out at the shining black water and try, insignificant little creature that he was, to make some sense of birth and death, and the frequent pain of the years between.

At such moments the captain always felt kinship with Candelmas, with that odd and ineluctable sense of grief he carried around with him like a ghostly companion.

The captain sailed on toward the round yellow moon that seemed suspended on the line of horizon just ahead.

II

IT TOOK THREE HOURS, but they found her. They were careful to keep her away from the sight of onlookers, spreading her charred black body out near one of the hose trucks, the firemen making a circle and blocking the view. She was examined quickly by two men in white medical smocks from the coroner's office, and then she was quickly put inside a body bag, placed on a stretcher, and carried to the boxy white ambulance where two bored-looking attendants had been waiting for her for nearly two hours. There wasn't much press here tonight. She had not been an important person and this was hardly an important neighbourhood. But by now there were four police cars and three fire trucks. The first group of neighbours had been joined by two or three other groups of neighbours, everybody wearing winter coats over pyjamas or flannel nightgowns. They had gone through sorrow, pity, a curious kind of remorse— maybe they should have smelled the smoke early and warned her somehow—and now they were in the process of becoming exhausted from so many big and helpless feelings. Yet they stayed, seemingly transfixed by the guttering flames and seared remains of the frame and foundation.

The fire inspector's name was O'Banyon. Meredith had been in the back seat of his official black Ford sedan for the past hour and fifteen minutes. He had been called away several times. Only now were they getting to talk at a leisurely and uninterrupted pace.

Meredith sipped the coffee O'Banyon had brought her. It tasted mostly of paper cup.

"Could we go over this one more time?" O'Banyon said. He was a somewhat overweight man in his early fifties. He wore a dark uniform. In the dome light Meredith could see that he also wore some kind of dye in his greying hair. She wondered why men's hair never looked natural when it had been tinted. O'Banyon took notes on an official-looking clipboard. "You were sitting in the living room with her."

"Yes."

"And you got up to go to the bathroom?"

"Right."

"Now, at this time did you smell any smoke?"

"No."

"All right, then. You went to the bathroom."

"Correct."

"And approximately how long had you been in there before you smelled smoke?"

"Five minutes, perhaps."

He grimaced. "That's what's so hard for me to grasp here."

"I know."

"You didn't smell any smoke whatsoever, yet five minutes later the entire house was engulfed in flames."

"Yes."

"Did you hear an explosion?"

"No."

O'Banyon made some more notes and sighed. "Mrs Frommer didn't mention any trouble she'd been having with her furnace, anything like that?"

"No."

He looked at her frankly. "If you had to speculate, what would you say happened?"

"I really don't have any knowledgeable opinion."

"I know. But sometimes people know more than they think."

Meredith shrugged. "It just—happened."

"Well, that's the hell of it. It didn't 'just happen.' Something made it happen."

Meredith felt as if he were almost accusing her of something.

She glanced out the side window. The number of onlookers had dwindled. Two of the big red fire trucks were backing out, leaving only one now. The press was nowhere in sight.

"Won't there be an investigation?" Meredith said.

"It's already started."

"And you haven't speculated on anything yourself'?"

He gave her a bashful grin that made him look much younger. "That's something we don't like to talk about."

"What's that?"

"Sometimes we can speculate all we want but we still don't know the cause of a fire. We look for the burning patterns—what we call V patterns—to see if the fire seems accidental or like arson. We look for heavy charring where it's not normally found and if we see enough of it, we get suspicious because it's likely that gasoline or some other flammable liquid is responsible for the areas of heavy charring. With an explosion, it's the same thing—common patterns that lead us to the answer. But sometimes—well, sometimes, no matter what we think happened, we can't prove it." He pointed his clipboard in the area of the smoking house. "I spent an hour looking around in there tonight."

"Did you form an opinion?"

He shook his head. "Not really. There doesn't seem to be any kind of common pattern. It doesn't look accidental but it doesn't look like arson, either. Of course, we'll keep going through the rubble with some people from the lab, but right now the fire doesn't suggest anything at all."

"It just started?"

He nodded. "It just started. And what makes no sense is that it seems to have started with no warning at all while you were in the bathroom. No sound of explosion. No screaming from Mrs Frommer until the flames were apparently covering her body." His eyes had narrowed now. He seemed to be studying her face. Again, she had the sense that she wasn't merely being questioned but was being put under close scrutiny as well. He sighed. "Well, if you don't have anything else to add, I guess we can call it a night."

"I appreciate all your help."

"I'm sorry about your friend."

"I appreciate that."

She got out of the car, drained the coffee, crumpled the cup, and shoved it into the pocket of her coat. She'd dispose of it later.

She took a last look at the remains of the house. She could still hear Mrs Frommer crying out. Meredith had been no help at all.

She turned and was walking down the street to her car when she saw it, the grey Volvo just now pulling away from the kerb.

She instantly flashed on the grey Volvo she'd seen earlier tonight in her parking lot. And the woman in dark glasses, seeming to stare up at Meredith.

The Volvo was headed in the opposite direction, so there was no chance for Meredith to see the face of the driver.

But somehow she knew it was the same woman who'd been outside her apartment earlier.

III

SHE WASN'T SURE what time the call came, After getting home from Mrs Frommer's, she'd taken a sleeping pill, knowing she'd need one, and also knowing that the pill would probably leave her with a drug hangover in the morning. But tonight she desperately needed sleep. She couldn't get Mrs Frommer from her mind, nor the sense that she'd somehow let the woman down.

When the phone woke her, she was groggy and disoriented.

"Hello," Meredith said after comically patting the shadows until her fingers reached the receiver.

She could tell that someone was there. But there were no words. Just faint breathing.

"Hello," Meredith said again. She tried to remember how many times you were supposed to say hello before hanging up. Ma Bell had very specific instructions for dealing with obscene or prank phone callers.

The caller surprised her. The caller hung up.

Meredith sat upright in the darkness. Chill wind whipped

against the windows. It sounded very much like Mrs Frommer's screams. She wondered about the phone call she'd just received. She had been thinking terrible thoughts tonight, ever since Mrs Frommer had brought up Dr Candelmas and Perpetual Light.

Even with the effects of the sleeping pill, it was nearly dawn before she got back to sleep.

IV

GAGE LOVED the Illinois countryside, the variegated landscape especially. Only half an hour from Chicago you started to see deep timberland and rolling hills. Now, in the last of autumn, the land had a mournful beauty that Gage appreciated on an emotional level. He was in mourning, too, as his psychotherapist kept reminding him. It'll just take time, my friend, the shrink always said; it'll just take time.

Gage was indulging himself and he knew it. He was still working the Jacob Myles homicide case and he found himself with a perfectly legitimate excuse for a drive in the country. He even had a sunny day to make it more beautiful.

Everybody he talked to about Myles brought up Perpetual Light. Even the elusive Meredith Sawyer admitted that the school had been her only contact with the man. But as yet, Gage had an imprecise understanding of Perpetual Light. What had it been exactly? Ostensibly, of course, it had been an orphanage. Dr Candelmas recruited the brightest children from orphanages throughout the Midwest and brought them to Perpetual Light. Meredith was an example of this.

Gage decided that actually seeing the place might help him. Plus, it was a great excuse to spend a few hours in the country.

As he drove he kept thinking of how Jacob Myles's body had been found in the alley, the top of his head little more than a hash of smashed bone and flesh. The only other case Gage could liken it to was a hammer killing he'd covered once on the South Side. He'd been unable to eat red meat for two weeks.

He turned off the highway onto an asphalt county road. He drove seven miles due south, crested a long hill, and there below him, in a deep, narrow valley, sat the remains of Perpetual Light.

The once magnificent stone main house had been burned to little more than charred foundation. Three other houses, similar in design and construction but much smaller, lay north of the main house. These had not been burned but they had been abandoned. Even from here Gage could see that all the windows had been smashed out and graffiti sprayed across the exterior walls. Farm equipment, now decades out-of-date, had been left to rust. It resembled metal sculptures of some ancient, forlorn race of beasts abandoned to the vagaries of time. Only the trees and farm fields surrounding Perpetual Light were alive.

Autumn had never looked brighter or more graceful —wide orange pumpkins in a patch along one edge of the property, and a scarecrow looking ridiculously like Ray Bolger at the other edge. Mighty black crows rose against the soft blue sky and smoky haze of the day. Pheasants perched on fenceposts to idly look things over.

He drove down there and got out.

The air was wonderful; chilly but fresh. He walked through an entrance gate. Vast black stone angels sat on pillars on either side of the gate, but they had been despoiled, their noses broken away, their breasts cleaved off. The closer he drew to the main house, the easier it was to imagine what the place must have been like in its glory, cars and trucks pulling up to the wide porch, staff and children delighted with the autumn day, laughter dying only as darkening day crept over the sunny hills.

But now there was just the wind, sounding lonely and hollow as it worked its way among the rubble of the main house.

He walked up the porch steps and opened the door. He was greeted not by a vestibule but by the sight of burned furnishings and toppled stones. A rat rested on a flat rock, a plump brave fellow who didn't seem the least intimidated by a city detective. He stared at Gage for a time, then went back to observing another part of the mansion.

Gage made his way inside the main house. He moved carefully. The rubble was precariously balanced and Gage could find himself pitched deep into the debris, breaking a leg or worse.

He spent the next half-hour combing through the rubble. If he was looking for anything in particular, he had no idea what it was. The clean scent of wind was not to be found within the remaining walls of the main house. Here you smelled only time-rotted wood and mud foetid with a variety of animals in various stages of decomposition and the faint smell of the burned foundation even after all these years.

If he was looking for nothing, that was exactly what he found.

Finished with the interior of the house, he climbed out, flipping a quick salute to his friend the rat.

He had just walked out the front door again when he saw the green Dodge sedan parked next to his own car. The Dodge was empty. A young man in red windbreaker and jeans was walking toward the main house.

The young man waved, as if to show that he was just as friendly as he looked. Gage waved back and started walking down the stairs.

"Morning," the young man said.

"Morning."

"My name's Conroy." He was blonde and slight with intelligent blue eyes. He looked to be in his early thirties. From his neck dangled a thirty-five-millimetre camera. "I'm with the county newspaper."

Gage shook hands with the man, telling him that he was a Chicago detective.

"Wow, I'm impressed," Conroy said. "A Chicago detective. That's worth writing a story about. You must be checking out Perpetual Light too."

Gage laughed. "Well, it would be worth a story if I were doing anything more than just looking around." Like most cops, he was reasonably skilled at protective coloration—he believed the nuns used to call it lying. "Needed to testify in a county case and was on my way back. Saw this and thought I'd have a look. I'm kind of an architectural freak. Plus, I've always heard about Perpetual Light." He stared out at the magnificent ruins of the place. "This must have been something in its heyday."

"Actually," Conroy said, "From what I hear, it was a cover."

"Oh? A cover for what?"

"You mean you never heard the rumours about its being a cult?"

"Perpetual Light was a cult? I thought it was an orphanage."

"That was the cover."

"Must have been some cover," Gage said. "I've never heard that rumour before."

Conroy shrugged. "I think it's kind of interesting."

Now Gage turned back to the main house and looked at it. "You know how stories get started."

"Sure; if you mean gossip and rumour."

"Bob Dylan said believe half of what you see and none of what you hear."

Conroy laughed. "Great. A cop who quotes Bob Dylan. I'll have to remember that." Then he became serious again. "You mean you think the cult story is just a myth?"

"Or at least highly exaggerated."

"Dr Candelmas, the man who ran this place, never wanted anything to do with townspeople."

"That doesn't make him a cult leader."

"But the people who came out here—tradesmen, mostly—said that when you looked at what some of these kids were doing well, it looked pretty strange."

"Such as what?"

"Oh, memorising cards with strange symbols on them."

"Strange symbols?"

"I've got drawings of some back at my office."

"Anything else?"

"Just a general air of strangeness, I guess."

A general air of strangeness, Gage thought. The same kind that got witches burned and gave rise to the Inquisition, strangeness largely being in the eye of the beholder.

"So why're you interested in Perpetual Light at this particular time?" Gage asked.

Conroy nodded to the pumpkin patch. "You're forgetting what time of year it is."

"Oh. Right. Halloween."

"Exactly." Conroy smiled again. "And what better time for a spooky story about a cult than this time of year?"

"I guess you've got a point there." Gage's eyes roamed the deserted grounds. Then he looked at Conroy. "But seriously, you don't believe these stories about a cult, do you?" He had a sense that the younger man had told him all this for his own reasons. Gage wasn't sure why.

"Oh, I don't know. I grew up around here. I'm so used to legends about Dr Candelmas and Perpetual Light that I almost hope they are true." He laughed. "I'd be awful disappointed if they weren't true."

"Well, I don't suppose we'll ever know now, one way or the other," Gage said.

But he had to admit that he was more suggestible than he liked to think, because ever since Conroy had started talking about a cult the grounds had taken on a sinister, shadowy look to Gage.

He said good-bye to Conroy and then got in his car and drove away. When he last saw Conroy, the newspaperman was down on one knee, taking a dramatic shot of the main house's front door.

V

AROUND NOON she decided she was pampering herself, so she got up, stumbled into the shower, and forced herself to come awake. Only vaguely did she remember calling Todd at the office and telling him that she'd be home today, describing the fire and poor Mrs Frommer.

For lunch she had a tuna fish sandwich and a glass of skim milk. As she ate she made plans for the afternoon. Ever since her visit with Mrs Frommer last night, she'd found herself curious about Perpetual Light again. In the back of her closet were two boxes packed with memorabilia. She'd spend the afternoon going through it all.

She was just putting the tuna fish back into the fridge when the yellow kitchen-wall phone rang.

She answered it automatically, without thinking.

"Hello?"

Nothing.

"Hello?"

Then she remembered last night's phone call.

"Dammit," she said, "I'm getting very tired of this."

She slammed the phone down and went into her bedroom to get dressed in jeans and a NORTHWESTERN sweatshirt. Then she'd get down to business with her Perpetual Light memories. Maybe by going through the box she'd find some clue as to why Mrs Frommer would have wanted to talk to Dr Candelmas.

She was just tugging her sweatshirt on when the phone rang again. This time she was smart. She didn't answer it.

VI

THE COMMANDER had recently attended a police seminar in San Diego. He returned filled with ideas for making his department the most efficient and effective in Chicago. Or so he told the men and women on his 'team' for something like two hours that afternoon.

In high school Gage had learned how to appear fascinated while secretly being tuned out. He focused his seemingly rapt attention on the commander and then proceeded to revisit Perpetual Light. Once more he wandered the ruins of the place. Once more he tried to imagine how splendid it must have been before the fire, like a southern plantation before the righteous flames of the Civil War. And now he tried to imagine what a teenage Meredith Sawyer must have looked like standing in the autumn sunlight, a red autumn apple in her supple white hand.

"...nothing less than revolutionise the way police work is done," the commander was saying. He was a man who seemed oblivious to the coughing, smirking, and eye-rolling of others. It was a good thing for him because this afternoon all three were in ample evidence.

Sensing that the commander was droning to a conclusion, Gage reluctantly brought himself back from the autumnal splendour of Perpetual Light.

"And speaking of good examples, look at Gage here. Why,

my God," the commander said, "This man hangs on every word you say. Every word. Right, Gage?"

"Uh, right, sir," Gage said. He felt his cheeks burn. He hadn't blushed in a long time.

He turned to look at his fellow officers. They were smirking again, only this time he was the object of their scorn, not the commander.

As soon as the meeting was finished, Gage headed straight for his battered desk to phone the offices of *Windy City*. For several reasons, he wanted to see Meredith Sawyer again.

VII

THE CHOPPER was a Hughes two-seater. As it descended to the stern of the yacht, its dome sparkled in the waning afternoon sunlight.

A tall, beefy man in a chocolate-brown suit and mirror sunglasses departed the chopper. The pilot, who likewise wore mirror shades, sat smoking a Viceroy and awaiting his employer's return.

The captain worked his way toward the chopper, holding on to his white hat against the wind created by the whirring blades.

The larger man put out his hand. The captain shook it, then led the man to the cabin and then below deck.

"He never changes, does he?" the large man said, noting the near night-like darkness of the cabin.

The captain smiled. "No, he never does."

The large man carried a briefcase. As the captain knocked and waited for a response from Dr Candelmas, the man checked through his papers once again, then snapped the briefcase shut.

"Come in," a voice said from behind the door.

"There you go," the captain said.

"Thanks."

The large man put his hand on the doorknob and went inside.

The stateroom was large and elegantly furnished. When touched by daylight, it was also probably beautiful. But in shadow, the Mediterranean furniture was sombre, funereal.

Dr Candelmas was stretched out on the couch. A Bach tape

played. Candelmas, wearing his familiar black robe, sat up and said, "Did you find her?"

The man smiled. "You never were much for amenities."

"According to myth, private investigators aren't much for amenities either. I thought you fellows relied on forty-fives and your fists."

Reynolds sat down, opened his briefcase.

"Here," Reynolds said. He took a manila envelope from his briefcase and set it on the table between them. "Why don't you look inside?"

Candelmas nodded. As always, he smelled tangy, of exotic and enormously expensive after-shave.

Even in the shadows, Reynolds could see that Candelmas's hands were trembling.

Candelmas opened the envelope and extracted four large black-and-white proof sheets.

He took the sheets over to one of the windows and pulled the curtain back.

He looked at each sheet carefully, then let the curtain fall. He came back to where Reynolds sat.

He handed the envelope back to Reynolds. The private investigator was starting to smile, satisfied that he'd just earned his spectacular fee, when Candelmas's large, powerful hand came out of nowhere and caught Reynolds so hard on the side of the face that the man was lifted up from his seat.

"You stupid son of a bitch," Candelmas said. "That isn't Emily at all."

5

I

AROUND THREE that afternoon Gage's phone rang. It was Dr Birnbaum from St. Michael's saying that his patient George Chesmore could talk now, "but I don't know if he will. I'll give you fifteen minutes with him if you'd like."

Gage thanked the doctor and drove over to the hospital. He

took the elevator to the fourth floor and was met, exactly at four o'clock, by Birnbaum.

"He's still not in very good shape," the doctor said as he led Gage down well-polished floors.

"Oh?"

"Very deep depression."

"Is it anything you can tell me about?"

The doctor stopped and shrugged. "He keeps talking about his old job."

"Which was what?"

"He was a counsellor at an orphanage called Perpetual Light."

The doctor pushed open the door to 427. The room smelled of flowers, like a funeral home. The drapes were half drawn. The light was grey, drab. A plump old man with white hair sat in a rumpled robe and pyjamas in a chair across from an unmade single bed. A reading light shone over the man's shoulder. The man was reading a Robert B. Parker paperback.

"George," Dr Birnbaum said.

George Chesmore looked up. He had the watery blue gaze of a very old man. "Hello, Dr Birnbaum."

"Hello, George."

"Do you remember that I mentioned a detective coming to see you."

George nodded. "Is this the man?"

"Yes, George. This is the man."

"I really don't want to talk to him very long, Dr Birnbaum."

"Don't worry. I told him that you're not really up to seeing visitors. He won't take much of your time."

Chesmore held up his Robert B. Parker paperback and looked at Gage. "I don't suppose police work is anything like this."

Gage smiled. "Not much, I'm afraid."

"I'll be back in a few minutes, George. I'll just be down the hall," Dr Birnbaum said.

George watched the doctor leave. He took a wrinkled white handkerchief from the pocket of his robe and daubed at his mouth. "I drool."

"Pardon me?"

George pointed a finger at his mouth. "I'm depressed all the time so they have to give me extra medication. And the medication makes me drool." He put his handkerchief back in his robe pocket and laid the paperback facedown on his lap. "I can't imagine why a policeman would want to talk to me. I'm a law-abiding citizen."

Gage told him about the bloody murder of Jacob Myles. He went easy on the gory details. He figured George didn't need any more help being depressed.

"We found a notebook on him," Gage said.

"Oh, yes, his famous notebook."

"'Famous notebook'?"

"We used to kid him about it. At Perpetual Light. He wrote everything down. Everything."

"Your name was in the notebook."

"It was?"

"Yes. And I wondered if you could tell me why."

"Not really. I haven't heard from Jacob in years. We were always pretty good friends, too. It's a shame the way people lose contact with each other."

"Yes, it is."

"But I don't know why Jacob would—" He shook his head. And touched long fingers to his temple. "Headache."

"Aspirin help?"

"Not really. I've had it ever since I started getting depressed."

"You mind if I ask why you're here?"

"I don't mind but I'm afraid it's going to sound pretty crazy."

"All right."

"All of a sudden I just wanted to kill myself."

"No specific reason?"

"Not really. I miss my wife. I lost her to heart disease a few years ago, but I don't think that's it."

"Does Dr Birnbaum have any explanation?"

"Not really."

"Have you actually tried to take your own life?"

"No; mostly I've just talked about it. But that made my sister very nervous. So I came here."

Gage paused. "Did you know Jacob Myles's personal habits?"

"Oh, some I suppose. He liked to play poker, I remember that. We used to call him 'Iron Butt' for how long he could sit at a card table."

"Did he drink much?"

"Not when I knew him."

"Run around with women a lot?"

"He was happily married."

"Wasn't a latent homosexual as far as you know?"

"Jacob? No way."

"And the last time you talked to him was approximately when?"

"Oh, fifteen years ago. He called me for lunch one day. Out of the blue."

"Did you go?"

"Met him over in Evanston."

"Did he say anything important?"

"Not really. He'd still been doing project work for Dr Candelmas after Perpetual Light was officially closed down. He just said that he was looking forward to getting out of Candelmas's clutches."

"Did that surprise you?"

"Good Lord, no. Everybody wanted out of Dr Candelmas's clutches."

"You included?"

"Of course. He was a very strange man. Very secretive." Just then, Chesmore touched his forehead with long fingers. He grimaced. "Damned headache. Dr, Birnbaum wants me to have some cranial X rays and a brain scan."

"Oh?"

"The headaches started just before the depression. Dr Birnbaum thinks there could be a relationship between the two. He says that sometimes depression can be the result of brain damage. I've never heard of that, have you?"

"No," Gage said, and smiled. "But then I'm not an M.D."

He stood up and put his hand out. "Thanks, Mr Chesmore."

"You're welcome. But I sure doubt that I helped you much." He tapped his paperback. "Spenser sure wouldn't be satisfied with an interview like this one."

Gage laughed. "No, he'd probably shoot you or fix you a gourmet meal. Or quote something literary to you."

"You've read him, then, huh?"

"I used to. He used to be the best."

On his way to the elevator, Gage saw Birnbaum and thanked him.

Just as the elevator doors were closing, the cry came from the floors above, and Gage imagined again a man trapped animal-like in a small cage and crying for help. Gage tried not to think of the small cage his marriage had become.

II

SHE HADN'T had a good long cry in months and she needed one.

She sat in the centre of her living room floor, surrounded by photos and letters and mementoes that described a life, her life, for the past thirty-one years. There were quite silly things such as birthday cards with floppy bunny ears and quite serious things such as her college diploma, the odds and ends of existence.

And then she found the photographs of her sister.

They didn't look much alike.

Valerie had been luxuriously blonde and devastatingly beautiful. She combined innocence and eroticism in equal measure. She had also been considerably smarter than Meredith. Before they'd gone to Perpetual Light, they'd attended a school where a sour old woman was always pitting them against each other. "Are you going to let your sister show you up again?" the teacher often asked. For a time Meredith had been jealous of Valerie. Who wouldn't be with a sister so clearly superior in every way? Valerie was even considered the nicest of the two girls, not being given to Meredith's dark moods or self-deprecating attitude. Not that Meredith was unblessed— she was quite nice-looking, smart, and a good friend even to people who were sometimes cruel to her. But she was not the glowing beauty, the dazzler, that Valerie had been. After Valerie's death, Meredith felt guilty about ever being jealous of her sister.

70

Hadn't Valerie always seen to it that Meredith was included in all the parties and games and larks with the most popular girls? Hadn't Valerie always been there to console her whenever Meredith started thinking about their parents, and sliding down into one of her moods? Hadn't Valerie almost been her parent sometimes as well as her sister and friend?

Now, lifting a photo of Valerie up to the waning daylight, Meredith thought again of her sister's last few months. Valerie had changed somehow. Gone was the intimacy they'd enjoyed; gone, too, was Valerie's lightheartedness, which Meredith had frequently relied on. Valerie stayed in bed a lot and shunned many of her friends. The few times Meredith asked her directly what was wrong, Valerie snapped that she was tired of always having Meredith around. One night, home early from a student concert, Meredith had entered their dark dorm room to hear Valerie on the top bunk, sobbing.

A few months later, the accident took place. A school car carrying three students and a faculty member skidded out of control on an icy road, pitched headfirst into a deep ravine, and burst into flames. All four people were killed.

Meredith had lost her family twice—first her parents when she was very young, and then her beloved sister when she was a teenager. She supposed that was why so many of her later relationships, especially the one with Roger the past three years, had all been tainted with desperation. She did everything to make the relationship endure, including letting Roger belittle her and virtually tell her how to run her life. Only through an incredible act of will had she been able to push away from Roger, and since then her only satisfaction was the strength she felt being her own person again. But for all that, she still felt lonely.

Near the bottom of the box she found more pictures of Perpetual Light people, including Mrs Frommer. Somebody had snapped Meredith's picture—she'd been about thirteen then—with Mrs Frommer's arm around her. Both of them looked young and vital and happy, and Meredith felt a curious pang for the girl she used to be.

Finally, she came upon a photograph of Dr Candelmas. She

71

was almost shocked by it. The photo showed him standing in front of the main house dressed in his usual black suit, his hair just then turning prematurely white. Inside his long arms he held three young female students, one of them Valerie. How beautiful and vibrant and happy she looked in this photo, the Valerie that men and women alike found so stunning.

She was staring at the photo when the phone rang.

She got up from the box and crossed the floor.

"Hello?"

"This is Detective Gage."

"Oh. Hi."

"I called your office and they said you'd taken the day off."

"Yes." She explained to him about the fire.

"I'm sorry."

"So am I," she said. "It was so strange. I hadn't seen Mrs Frommer in years. Then I go over there and—"

Then she looked out the window to the parking lot below.

A grey Volvo was parked across the lot. Behind the wheel was a woman in a head scarf wearing dark glasses. Dusk was nearly here and the afternoon had been overcast anyway. Why would she need to wear dark glasses?

"I'm sorry," she said. "I'm afraid I got distracted."

"I asked if it would be all right if I came over."

"Oh, gosh," she said. "I'm really not dressed very well or anything. And the apartment's sort of a mess and—"

"How about letting me take you out for some food, then?"

"Seriously?"

"Seriously. You like Chinese?"

"I love Chinese."

"Why don't you take an hour and get ready and by that time I'll be there."

She turned away from the window. "Actually, that sounds nice."

He laughed. "Yes, it does, doesn't it?" He had a warm, masculine voice and it felt good in her ear.

"About an hour, then." She hung up.

She walked straight from the living room into the bedroom. She went into the walk-in closet, stood up on tiptoes, and flailed

72

her hand around near the back of the shell At first she didn't find anything. Eventually, though, her fingers touched expensive leather and she knew she'd found them.

The field glasses had been a gift from Roger for a vacation they'd taken in the Rockies.

She took them from their leather case, put them to her eyes, adjusted them, and then walked back into the living room.

She wanted a closer look at the woman in the grey Volvo. She also wanted a closer look at the Volvo's licence number.

She went to the window and started to bring the field glasses to her eyes.

But the grey Volvo and the woman in the sunglasses were gone.

III

"DR CANDELMAS, please."

"Who's calling?"

"Tell him Conroy. I edit the county paper and keep an eye on the place for him."

"This is the captain. You can give me a message and I'll make sure he gets it."

Conroy sighed. Five years ago, just after he'd graduated from the University of Illinois, he'd been out at the ruins of Perpetual Light one summer day when a long black limo pulled up. A chauffeur who looked more like a boxer had got out and asked him what he was doing on this land. Couldn't he see that it was posted PRIVATE?

Conroy had gotten scared. He had the feeling that the chauffeur would love to beat his face in.

The back window of the limo rolled down. All the windows were tinted. A man with white hair and a wide face and startling dark eyes leaned out. He appeared to be wearing a black silk robe and black silk pyjamas. He said to Conroy, in a no-nonsense voice, "Come over here."

"Yessir."

"Who are you?"

"Rick Conroy."

"And what are you?"

"Occupation, you mean, sir?"

The man nodded imperiously.

"Journalist."

"My," the man said. "One doesn't expect to meet a 'journalist' out in the boonies. And whom do you work for? Time or CBS or NBC?"

"No, sir, I work for the local paper."

Conroy couldn't stop himself from trembling. He just had the sense that something terrible was going to happen to him. The man in the limo was somehow unearthly.

"And you do what for the local paper?"

"Oh, cover stories. Things like that."

"Weddings?"

"Yessir."

"And barn raisings."

"Yessir."

"And 4-H shows."

"Yessir."

The man seemed amused. "How much do you make?"

"Seventy-two hundred a year, sir."

"Are you aware that's below the national poverty line?"

"Yessir. But Mr Hodges said he'd give me a raise if I stick it out a year."

"Sounds like a generous man."

"Yessir."

"How would you like to make a thousand dollars a month on the side? Every month."

"Are you kidding, sir?"

"I very rarely 'kid' about anything, young man."

"Yessir."

"Well, what's your answer?"

"I'd very much like to make a thousand dollars a month on the side. Depending on what I have to do, of course."

"Of course."

"And what would that be, sir?"

The man leaned farther out the limo window and waved his hand around to indicate the breadth of Perpetual Light. "I want

74

you to keep an eye on this for me."

"An eye?"

"I'll give you a phone number. You tell me if anybody seems unduly interested in this place. Or starts to snoop around. I don't care about teenagers out to smash a few windows, but I do care about people who seem seriously interested in the place. You being at the newspaper, you're in an ideal spot to know who's making inquiries."

"Yessir."

"All you have to do is phone me with any information you have and you'll receive a thousand a month. And tell no one else of the bargain we've struck."

"I can hardly believe this, sir."

"Well, you should believe it, young man, because it's true." The man leaned his head in the direction of the chauffeur. "Give him a down payment, Dennis."

The chauffeur nodded. From inside his grey uniform he took a long leather wallet. He soon laid a crisp thousand-dollar bill in Conroy's hand.

"Wow," Conroy said, knowing how young he sounded.

"Now give him the phone number, Dennis."

After Dennis had handed Conroy a small white business card, the chauffeur walked back to the front of the car, got in, started the engine again, and pulled away. The tinted back seat window went up. The limo sped away, pluming chalky dust.

From then on, promptly on the twelfth of every month, Rick Conroy received a white envelope with a crisp thousand-dollar bill in it. It always came to the newspaper office and he always took it straight home to his trailer and put it under the mattress with the others. By now he had a black Lab named Jake. Jake would take care of anybody foolish enough to try and get into the trailer.

In five years he'd called the number on the business card exactly three times.

This was the fourth. "The message?" the man who'd identified himself as the captain said again.

"Well, there was a Chicago detective named Gage out at Perpetual Light this morning. He asked a lot of questions. I told him all the local tales, you know, how it was actually a cult and everything, and then he went away."

"Anything else?"

"Not really."

"And he didn't give any indication of why he'd come out all the way from Chicago?"

"No, sir."

"Well, if you see him again, or hear from him, you be sure to call Dr Candelmas immediately."

The connection went woofy for a moment. Conroy recognised it as typical ship-to-shore transmission difficulties.

"You'll call immediately, then?" the captain repeated.

"Yessir, if I see or hear from him again."

"Thank you. I'll give this message to Dr Candelmas right now."

Conroy hung up and smiled. He didn't have a bad job here. Four phone calls in five years and he'd collected nearly sixty thousand dollars so far, and he hadn't reported a dime of it to the IRS.

Not a bad job at all.

He grabbed his hat and hurried on over to the feed-and-grain. The boys always had coffee at this time of day, and Conroy had recently become one of the boys after many years of trying.

IV

BY THE TIME Gage got there, Meredith was wearing a freshly ironed white blouse, designer jeans, and a pair of bulky argyle socks. She was afraid she might have overdone her perfume.

Five minutes before the detective's arrival Meredith was in the kitchen brewing fresh coffee. The aroma was friendly in the empty apartment.

She watched him leave his car and disappear downstairs in the entranceway. No sign whatsoever of a grey Volvo.

He knocked twice and she let him in.

"Well," he said, looking around. "This really suits you. All the bookcases and the TV set and the big map of Chicago in the 1800s. Very, very nice."

76

Closing the door, she took his all-weather coat and hung it in the hallway closet. "Care for some coffee?"

"Love some."

"Black?"

"Great."

By the time she returned, Gage was seated on the couch, poring through a book on Chicago history. "The first McDonald's was in Des Plaines?"

"Absolutely."

"I didn't know that."

She smiled and set his coffee down on the glass coffee table. "That's why you should subscribe to our magazine."

He smiled back. "Believe me, I will."

She took a seat in the chair across from him. They spent a long minute blowing on their coffee and tentatively sipping it, and then he said, "In the last week I've met some interesting people."

"I'd think you'd meet interesting people every day."

"A special kind of interesting people, I should say."

"Oh?"

"Yes, they all worked at Perpetual Light."

"I see." She could feel her body tense and her voice grow cold.

"You don't much like that subject, do you?"

"I suppose not."

"Care to tell me why?"

"Unhappy memories."

He laughed softly. "A detective could mistake you for an uncooperative witness."

"Really?"

"Sure. The last time we talked, I had the distinct impression that you were holding something back."

"I was."

"Care to tell me what?"

She blew on her coffee and thought a moment. "Perpetual Light. I never want to talk about it."

"Must have been pretty bad."

"My sister—she died while we were there."

77

"I'm sorry."

"So I guess I associate the place with her death."

"How long were you there?"

"Twelve years."

"It was an orphanage, right?"

"Right."

"A newspaperman named Conroy tells me that it was also considered something of a cult."

She laughed. "That's the story the townspeople like to tell, anyway. Every time we'd go into town—well, I suppose there was something just a little strange about most of us anyway, being orphans and all, and being very afraid of the turns our lives would take."

"The townspeople didn't like you?"

"They hated us. They'd sort of huddle together and stare and point and smirk. A few times some of the younger boys would even throw rocks at us."

"They must have thought you were pretty terrible people."

"They did. The county attorney was always trying to find some way to close Dr Candelmas down."

"Candelmas was—who?"

"The founder and the one man who controlled everything."

"Why did the county attorney want to shut him down?"

"Oh, he said that Dr Candelmas didn't teach state approved courses and that our degrees would be worthless—and he accused Dr Candelmas of teaching 'inappropriate' subjects."

"Such as what?"

She laughed again. "Science fiction movies. I must have seen *This Island Earth* about two hundred times while I was at Perpetual Light."

"Why did he show you science fiction movies?"

"He said he wanted to get us out of 'mental ruts' and see human potential for what it was. When I first got there, he was a very friendly and comforting man. But he changed over the years."

"Changed how?"

"For one thing, he wouldn't speak to most of the students. He seemed to be completely preoccupied. For another, he had

78

a fourth floor built onto the main house and he spent all his time there. There was a rear entrance with an elevator, so after a while we hardly saw Dr Candelmas at all."

"What went on on the fourth floor?"

"We never knew."

"You couldn't even guess?"

"Not really. Dr Candelmas insisted on strict secrecy."

"You sound as if you blame the school for your sister's death."

"In a way, I do. A school staff member was driving the car that went into the ravine. I think it's fair to hold him accountable, don't you?" She sounded a trifle defensive.

"It's natural, anyway, even if it isn't necessarily fair," Gage said.

"I just can't think of Perpetual Light without thinking of seeing my sister in the body bag being hauled up from the ravine."

"I'm sorry you had to talk about this."

"It's all right—it was on my mind already, anyway."

"Oh?"

She nodded and told him about the fire at Mrs Frommer's.

"She didn't say why she wanted to talk to you?"

"She said she needed my help in locating Dr Candelmas," Meredith said.

"That's strange." And then he told her about finding Chesmore's name in Myles's notebook and about Chesmore's depression and ending up in the mental hospital. "And the common element to all these people—you included—is Perpetual Light."

"That is odd." She shook her head. "I just keep thinking about poor Mrs Frommer."

"I'm sure they'll find some cause for the fire."

"If only I could have helped her."

Her phone rang. She leaned over and picked it up. "Hello."

The silence once again.

She sighed, cupping the phone. "Somebody who likes to play games."

She held the receiver a moment longer, listening, and then dropped it back on its cradle.

"Why don't you tell me about these calls on the way to the

restaurant?"

"Is that a hint?"

He patted his stomach. "I know I need to lose some weight, but that doesn't seem to stop me from getting hungry."

She patted herself on the bottom and smiled. "Me either."

She was walking past the living room window, on the way to the closet to get their coats, when she saw it. The tail end of a grey Volvo. Pulling away.

"Damn," she said. "I came this close."

"To what?"

She looked at him, exasperated. "To having a policeman verify the fact that I'm not just imagining things."

"Huh?"

She reached into the closet and got their coats. "C'mon. I'll explain it all over egg-rolls."

V

THIS TIME the punks didn't bother Croft. They smirked at him and one of them glowered at him in a way that was almost comic, but they made no moves on him. They remembered the other day, of course. They didn't know what had happened, they just knew that Croft was a strange man with some strange abilities. So they let him walk to and from the supermarket, untouched.

When he got back home, his arms weary from carrying the two sacks of groceries, he wondered again if he shouldn't get himself one of those little pull carts or even wagons. A cart would make lugging groceries a lot easier. But somehow that didn't square with his self-image. He'd never considered himself a macho man, but somehow a cart or a wagon would rob him of dignity. He'd rather have weary arms.

He locked the place up tight, four locks in all, and then he took his ancient gun from a desk drawer and put it up on the dining room table where he could get to it quickly. He knew he couldn't rely on any of the powers stress sometimes brought out. Sometimes the magic worked and sometimes it didn't.

It had been happening again—the same thing that had started

happening last week—and in case something happened he wanted to be ready.

Dusk turned his windows winter purple. He closed the drapes and turned on the network news. He hated all three of the pretty-boy news readers and so he alternated nights among CBS, NBC, and ABC. Give him Cronkite any day.

Dinner was a can of Campbell's chicken noodle, a piece of toast, and a cup of tea.

After this, he took his nightly bath.

Twenty years ago he'd injured his hip in a fall on an icy sidewalk. The doctor gave him pills and told him to start soaking in a hot bath every night. Since then, Croft had rarely missed a night. Nothing relaxed him like a bath.

He ran the water till it was just right—reading the new issue of *Time* on the john while the water ran—and then put his skinny white old man's body deep into the water.

It was wonderful.

He spent the first half hour in the tub finishing off *Time*. There were several pretty girls in this issue—face it, every magazine in the United States had become a skin magazine except maybe for *Reader's Digest*—and even at his age he liked to dote on them, wish he'd got married after all. But the years at Perpetual Light had taken his youth and before he knew it—

This time it sneaked up on him.

The times before, six times in all during the past six days, it had entered his mind like a jolt and demanded his attention immediately.

But this was more insidious, like a radio playing faintly, faintly.

The first sign that something was wrong was his body temperature. He was starting to sweat. Heavily.

The second sign that something was wrong was the faint wisp of steam rising off the bathwater. No way it should be that hot.

By then, of course, he had figured out what was about to happen, but it was too late.

His frail hands grasped the sides of the bathtub, but no matter how much strength he put into his fingers, they would not help raise him up out of the water.

81

He next tried standing up and leaping out of the tub, but that didn't work either. No matter how much he tried to raise his buttocks from the bottom of the tub, they remained stuck to it.

He sat there, horrified, and watched the water start to bubble.

At first he thought it might be an optical illusion, the way the surface of the water had begun to pop.

But the steam told him it was no illusion. The steam had a definite shape now and rose like wraiths from the surface of the water.

He tried lifting himself up and out, but it was still no use.

So he sat there and cried for help and thought of all the times he could have introduced himself to his other neighbours in this apartment house but did not. He was not a snob, Croft, nor was he undone by the fact that he was the only white man in this apartment house. But he was not an outgoing man and when he was around strangers he became so shy, he could barely meet their eyes.

So now he sat in a tub of water that was beginning to bubble and pleaded for the mercy of strangers.

He wasn't sure at what point his cries became screams. Probably around the time the water began reaching boiling point.

He threw his arms over the sides of the tub and tried to grab on to the sink for purchase.

For an exhilarating moment, he thought his fingers would reach. They came close, so close, to the sink. He could see himself pulling his body from the water, just in time before the water started to—

The water was now turbulent beyond belief. It seethed with heat.

He stretched, stretched to reach the sink—

And he had almost reached there when—

He felt a long muscle pull somewhere along his side.

The stretching had torn it.

He tried to wiggle his fingers closer to the sink, but the muscle pain was blinding.

He slipped back into the tub of seething water and once again started screaming for help. .

There was a certain fascination in watching the turbulent water. The noise it made now was almost deafening.

He knew he didn't have much longer. This kind of heat would inflict third-degree burns over most of his body.

At Perpetual Light, he had learned to summon his powers. And how to use them. But he had also learned that people with superior powers could block his. And right now that's what the sender was doing.

Croft could feel his own powers rising within him the way they had the other day with the street punk, a superior set of powers was rendering his useless.

He had a funny thought: He would rather have died at the hands of those black punks than die this way. At least he would have had his clothes on. Nakedness made you so vulnerable...

He saw the flesh around his ribs go first. It started welting up, as if a leather belt had just cracked across it. The pain was astonishing.

He cried out once more, a friendless man in a friendless world.

The process didn't take much longer. His entire body became rash red from the burns, and because he was not a strong man anyway, his face was soon beneath the water. He drowned before the burns could take him.

After a time, the water ceased being troubled, and was still and cool once more.

Croft lay beneath it, head turned in three-quarter profile, a single blue eye staring straight up at the ceiling where the plaster needed fixing.

It would have been better to die at the hands of the punks.

VI

CANDELMAS SAID, "I want you to put into shore."

"All right," the captain said. He paused. "You look tired, sir."

"I am tired."

"The private detective did not have good news?" They were in Candelmas's cabin. The drapes drawn. That peculiar twilight Candelmas liked. "He thought he did."

"Meaning what, sir?"

"Meaning I'm not up to chatting with the help."

"Yes, sir." The captain tried to scour any hurt from his voice. As an Annapolis graduate, he liked to think he could endure the snub of a superior.

"I'm sorry."

"Sir?"

"Sorry for making that remark."

"Yessir."

"You're a good man, Captain, and I appreciate all you do for me."

"Thank you, sir."

"Now let's put into shore."

"Yes, sir."

The captain snapped a salute and then started to the door. He thought of what two of the crew had told him this morning. About the sounds coming from Candelmas's room last night. Sobbing.

Could it really have been Candelmas sobbing?

He thought of the fact that Candelmas had just apologised to him. That was extraordinary for the man, apologising.

Perhaps the stories about sobbing weren't all that impossible, then.

The captain opened the door, closed it quietly behind him, and then mounted the stairs to the deck.

VII

ALL THE WAY over to the restaurant she kept glancing in Gage's rear-view mirror.

Finally he said, "You seem to be under the impression that somebody's following us."

"Somebody is."

"You really think so?"

"About half a block back. A grey Volvo sedan."

He squinted into the rear-view mirror. Dusk was thick now, neons and car lights bobbing like buoys in the ocean of darkness. "Afraid I can't pick it out."

"Wait till we move away from this stoplight. You'll see."

"How long has the car been back there?"

"Ever since we left my apartment."

He smiled. "You missed your calling."

"It's not as big a deal as you think. She's been sitting out in my parking lot for days."

"Do you have any idea why?"

"None whatsoever."

"Has she threatened you in any way?"

"Nope."

"I'll be damned," he said.

Gage kept flicking his eyes back to the rear-view every chance he got. The grey Volvo was unfailingly about half a block behind them.

"You ever get a good look at her?" he said.

"Not really. She always wears a head scarf and dark glasses."

"Sunglasses?"

"Right."

Gage's eyes went to the rear-view again. They were at another stoplight. Meredith looked around. The rush hour was in full swing. All the men and women in their business suits and overcoats looked impatient to get home. Kick their shoes off. Sit in front of the TV with their feet up on the ottoman. Eat something warm and satisfying for dinner.

Gage screeched off the line like a teenager showing off his new Trans Am.

Meredith was thrown back in her seat. "Watch those g-forces," she said, laughing.

"Thought I'd shake her up a little," Gage said, keeping his foot close to the floor. "Make her work for it."

Meredith turned her head slightly so she could see the grey Volvo try to keep up with Gage.

At first they seemed to have lost the Volvo entirely. No sight of it at all.

But about three blocks down, just as Gage was taking a sharp corner on what felt like two wheels, the Volvo appeared again. It was coming fast. Catching up.

"Hang on!" Gage said.

The next four blocks were a breathless blur. Somehow Gage managed to swerve in and out of traffic without getting into an accident. Cars honked; drivers swore and shook fists.

"It's a good thing you're a cop," Meredith said above the screech of Gage's tires. "Otherwise you could get arrested!"

"This is my own car," Gage shouted back, putting the accelerator to the floor now that they were racing along a side street that paralleled the river. He glanced over at her and grinned. "And I could get arrested."

The Volvo appeared again.

The woman was going at least as fast as Gage.

She seemed to swoop up out of nowhere and then challenge Gage for the right to use this deserted side street.

Gage held tight to the wheel to keep the car from rolling over.

The grey Volvo drew a bead on the exact centre of Gage's car and came directly at him.

For just a moment, a terrible moment, Meredith glimpsed the woman behind the Volvo's steering wheel. Black glasses. Head scarf.

Gage whipped the wheel hard to the right, skidding the car up over the kerb just as the Volvo made its move to broadside the Buick.

The Volvo missed Gage's car by inches. If she'd hit them as she'd planned, there was a good chance that both Meredith and Gage would be dead now.

The Volvo roared past them, vanishing around a corner half a block ahead.

"Well, one thing you can be sure of," Gage said as the Buick jumped the kerb and he slammed on the brakes.

"What's that?"

"You weren't imagining her. She's very real. And that's for sure."

Snow started spitting from the sky about the time their food was served. Even this light snowfall made Meredith melancholy. Snow always had this effect on her. She sat in the booth, staring out at the flakes sparkling as they passed through the yellow illumination of the parking lot lights and then vanishing into the cold darkness.

"Are you all right?"

She turned away from the window and looked at Gage. She liked looking at Gage. Again, while he wasn't a movie star, he had a nice, comfortable masculine face.

"Snow always gets to me."

"Rain does it to me."

"Really?"

"Right before a storm? You know how you can smell the rain? I always get a little scared, like something terrible is going to happen. My dad says I got lost in a park just before a storm hit and that they had a hard time finding me. It must be from that. The way I get scared, I mean."

She looked at him and smiled. "You're sure a nice guy, Detective Gage."

"And you're sure a nice woman, Meredith Sawyer."

She hesitated. "Gage?"

"Yes, ma'am."

"There's one thing we need to talk about."

"A woman in a grey Volvo?"

"No."

"Somebody who keeps calling you but hangs up?"

"I'm serious, Gage. It's about your marriage."

She saw the sorrow immediately. It was almost as if he'd forgotten the reason for the pain, but now that she'd reminded him the sorrow came back relentlessly. She almost regretted bringing it up, but she didn't want to get involved with a married man. And she did feel that in some way, they were getting involved.

"I knew we were going to get around to it eventually," he said.

"It's that painful?"

"That painful."

"I'm sorry, Gage."

"No, it's all right. Why don't we just get it out of the way now, once and for all?"

87

"You're sure."

"I'm sure." He laughed softly. "Then I can play cop and ask you a lot of questions about the grey Volvo and these strange phone calls."

She decided to say it then. "And Perpetual Light."

"Oh?"

She nodded. "You remember when you said that you had the sense I was holding something back?"

"Right."

"Well, I was. There are some things I need to tell you about the school. And about Dr Candelmas."

He stared right at her and she could see the unmistakable affection in his eyes. "Ladies first?"

"No. Why don't you go first." She giggled. "I'm chicken."

So he spent the next half hour telling her about his marriage.

Dessert was a small wedge of apple pie. "A fitting end to a Chinese dinner." He laughed.

She understood him now that he'd told her about his marriage. She hoped she'd similarly told him a few things about herself by describing her long and ultimately disastrous relationship with Roger.

"Well," he said, "It doesn't sound as if either one of us did very well in the romance department."

"I don't plan to give up trying."

"Neither do I."

And they toasted each other with their cups of coffee, as patrons around them watched and smiled.

And then the headache stabbed through her forehead.

"What's wrong?" he said.

"Headache."

"Must be bad, huh?"

She had to squint. Somehow it felt better with her eyes closed. "It's like the worst ice-cream headache in the world times one hundred."

"Want me to get you some Bufferin or something?"

"Would you please?"

"Be right back."

She put her head far forward into her hands. For a long moment she was able to block out light and sound and drift in the star-speckled darkness.

Faintly, she heard the sounds she always associated with these headaches. She thought of a 33-rpm record album played as 16 rpm—the words slow, incomprehensible. But the point was… they were words and she wondered what they were saying.

Gage was back within two minutes.

With his thumb he slit off all the safety packing on the Anacin, knocked out two white tablets into the palm of her hand, and then raised her glass to her mouth. "Later on I make chicken soup."

She smiled. "I'll bet you make good chicken soup."

She took the two tablets.

"You want to get out of here?"

"No. Sitting here's fine. In fact, I'm enjoying it very much."

"May I take that as a compliment?"

"You may indeed."

The restaurant continued to get busier. Busboys were running into waitresses. Patrons packed the front of the restaurant, waiting for their names to be called so they could finally be seated. Waiters did not walk around, they jogged.

Meredith touched her long fingers to her forehead. "The funny thing is, I associate these headaches with Perpetual Light."

"Really?"

"Um-hm. They're a special kind of headache." She then explained how the pain seemed to are down the exact centre of her forehead and how voices sounded just on the edge of her hearing.

"Voices?"

She laughed. "Yes, and next thing you know, I'll be telling you about being abducted by UFOS."

"But the voices are strange."

She nodded. "These headaches started when I was fifteen or so. They went away for a long time, but over the past couple of years they've come back."

"Have you ever talked to a doctor about them?"

"Many times."

"And?"

She shrugged. "Nothing, really. He just said that hearing voices isn't all that uncommon, that it's often just the unconscious spilling over to the conscious, and that my headaches may mean that some day I'll suffer from migraines. But I hope not. My sister Valerie had migraines and they were horrible. Some days they were so bad, she couldn't even get out of bed."

"Your voice changes whenever you talk about Valerie."

"Really?"

"It gets softer. You must really miss her."

"I think about her all the time. You know, what Valerie would be doing now. Would she be married? Would she have children? What would she be wearing? What books would she like? I just wonder what she would be doing with her life."

"I'm just glad for you that you had your time together."

"I just wish it could have been at somewhere other than Perpetual Light," Meredith said.

He smiled. "Your voice changes when you mention that place, too."

"I'm afraid to hear how."

"Your voice gets tighter, and you bite your words off. You're angry."

"You must study voices."

"I do. It helps when I'm questioning people. I watch their eyes and I listen to the way they say things. Sometimes those are much more telling than what they actually say."

"Well, I don't try to hide my feelings about Perpetual Light, that's for sure. Dr Candelmas was just so…" She shook her head. "It's difficult to describe. He wanted to be father and mother and sister and brother. He wanted us to love and honour him in a way we couldn't. I mean, now I can see that it was his own need to be loved—that's why he made such a big thing of us paying him total respect. But it wasn't a very healthy atmosphere."

"How did the stories about the cults get started?"

"I suppose because of the A Group."

"What was that?"

"A group of his special students. The best according to Dr Candelmas. There were only five of them. He took them everywhere. Usually in a special van. He even made them dress alike, the kind of uniform you saw in Catholic schools. Blue jumpers and white blouses for the girls, and blue blazers and white shirts and blue trousers for the boys."

"You weren't one of them?"

"Hardly. I was a little bit of a rebel where Dr Candelmas was concerned. I just didn't want to get involved in all that smothering love that Dr Candelmas and his A Group seemed to share."

"How about Valerie?"

"Oh, she was definitely a member of the group. She worshiped Dr Candelmas. Literally, I'm afraid. I always attributed her feelings to the fact that we'd never known our own father and that Dr Candelmas became her surrogate father. Cheap armchair psychology, I know, but there wasn't any other way to explain it, how she went on and on about him, I mean. Once she even told me that she thought she was in love with him. I looked at her. I thought she was kidding me. But she wasn't. Then I realised how strange things had gotten with Dr Candelmas. And we kind of drifted apart over it. I kept telling her that she should lead a more normal life."

"Group A took up most of her time?"

"All, of her time. Those five kids, they—I blamed Dr Candelmas, of course. He could have seen to it that they led normal lives—as normal as you could lead in an orphanage, anyway—but it was too flattering for him to let go. Having these five teenagers follow you around and absolutely hang on every word you said. You should have seen him with them. He was like this proud father with his children. There was always something sad and withdrawn about Dr Candelmas—but he changed when he had the Group with him."

"Did you ever keep track of any of them?"

"Three of them died in the car wreck."

"Including Valerie?"

"Yes."

"I'm sorry. I didn't mean to bring that up again." He sighed, and reached over and touched her hand.

She liked the feel of his fingers and let them rest there. "As for the other two, I haven't seen them in years. I don't know what they're doing or where they are or anything."

He let his hand linger a moment longer and then withdrew it. "And no word from Dr Candelmas?"

"Oh, no. I wasn't exactly his favourite student." Then she touched her fingers to her forehead and said, "The headache."

"It's gone?"

"Yes."

"The miracle healing powers of Anacin."

"It's incredible."

"How about a walk in the snow to celebrate?"

She smiled, happy that the headache was gone, happy that she would no longer have to talk about Perpetual Light.

"You're on," she said.

She wasn't sure when the words deep in her subconscious began to speed up slightly and become more intelligible.

Maybe it was when they reached the edge of the river and looked out across the chill black water to the lights of expensive condominiums on the other side.

Maybe it was when they walked down past the gazebo and he lifted her up to pet a tiny kitten who looked frozen, crouched on the very tip of a tree limb.

Or maybe it was when they were walking back to the car and he brushed against her and she formed an image of what it would be like to kiss him. Nothing overtly sexual; just a tender kiss of friendship. She'd needed companionship for so long...

Anyway, whenever they first sounded, the words were actually words this time. Not simply sounds.

"You all right?" he asked as they walked back to the restaurant in the pale light of the quarter-moon.

"Yes," she said. "Just listening to the night."

"I'm listening to the night, too, and you know what it's telling me?"

"What?"

He put on a granny voice. "I'm cold as hell; I'm cold as hell."

She swatted him on the arm, the way teenage girls often swat their dates.

"Hey, that's a good right hook."

"Thank you," she said.

And then he kissed her.

He turned her gently toward him and before she even had time to think, she angled her face up to his and closed her eyes. And he kissed her.

It was the tender kiss she'd hoped for, not the urgent one of passion.

She felt weak anyway. She hadn't been kissed in so long, she felt like a swooning teenager.

She began to slide her arm around his middle.

And then: words. Words that she could almost understand; words that were like teasing whispers.

Words that disturbed her and ultimately ruined the kiss.

What were the words saying?

"Meredith."

Why were they now—after all these years—words she could almost understand?

"Meredith. Can you hear me?"

She had a sudden impression of cold. And then of a sharp pain in the back of her neck. And then of something poking her near the base of her spine.

"Meredith, I'm going to help you up now. All right?"

But the noises Gage made were faint. Imposed on them were the words that roared inside her mind, begging to be audible, understood.

Some of the coldness went away. She no longer felt anything poking her in the base of her spine.

And then someone was lifting her. Carrying her. But who? And why?

She had felt this dizzy and confused only once before, after a large mare had pitched her off the side and she'd slammed her head into the hard ground.

Carrying her…

"Meredith?"

"Yes."

"Who am I?"

"Silly. You know who you are."

"I want to hear you say it."

"Gage. You're Gage."

"All right. And what's the name of the magazine you work for?"

"You know that, Gage."

"Yes. But I want you to tell me. Please. It's important."

"The name is *Windy City*."

Gage sighed and sat back.

Suddenly, almost as if waking from a dream, she became aware of everything around her.

Car. Heater. Wind at window. Radio on but very, very low.

"What happened?" she said.

"I must be more of a powerhouse kisser than I realised." He smiled and took her hand. He was behind the wheel, she was on the passenger's side. "I'm afraid I don't actually know what happened. I just got very scared."

"We were kissing and—"

"And you slipped away. It wasn't as if you fainted. Not exactly anyway. It was more as if something were taking the strength from you and you began to crumple a little bit at a time. Unfortunately, you hit your head on the ground before I could grab you."

"That's why the goose egg," she said, touching the back of her skull.

"And then your back landed on the point of a sharp rock."

She felt her back. It hurt as if it had been stuck with a sharp stick.

"What happened?" he said.

"Words."

"Words?"

"They just filled my head all of a sudden."

Things started looking strange again—Gage's features green in the light of the dashboard, the tree limbs like skeleton fingers clawing at the dark night—so she closed her eyes again for a brief rest.

The words were gone now.

Just the wind soughing, soughing against the car.

"Maybe you'd better see a doctor," Gage said.

"I'll be all right."

"You sure?"

She opened her eyes again. "I'd like to go home and get in my jammies, I guess. If that'd be all right."

"As long as I can phone you at least once later on to see how you're doing."

"That would be nice, actually."

Gage started the car and took her home.

VIII

CANDELMAS SAT in the rear of the limo, looking at Lake Shore Drive play across the broad windshield like images on a drive-in movie screen. The John Hancock Centre, the Water Tower Place, and, in the distance, the Chicago Tribune Tower rose against the wintry sky like arrogant idols proclaiming their dominion over all below.

Next to him, the woman started to cry again. Her name was Ellen Frazier. As a girl she had been one of Perpetual Light's most brilliant students. Now Candelmas hoped she could find Emily for him.

"I'm not going to hurt you, dear, when are you going to understand that?" Candelmas's voice could not quite hide his irritation, yet it strained to sound pleasant and paternal.

She wore a dark suit, a dark coat, and a dark hat with a long veil that completely obscured her face. She looked as if she were prepared to attend a very formal funeral. Her perfume, ironically, was lovely.

Behind the veil, she continued to cry. "Didn't Arlan talk to you? Didn't he tell you what we wanted? That we're just looking for Emily to help her?"

The hat and veil nodded.

"Then you know that we don't in any way mean to harm you, don't you see?"

The hat and veil nodded again.

95

Sometimes oncoming car lights played across her veil and Candelmas could almost see her face. Almost. But Arlan said that she was adamant. Nobody was to see her face. Under any circumstances. Nobody. Ever. Candelmas had no choice but to comply. The experiments had not gone well and Candelmas of course blamed himself to some degree. So, whenever he had to use her powers to locate people, he honoured her request about the veil.

After a time, the woman calmed down.

Candelmas sat back in the broad, deep seat. He sat close to her, as if they were quite good friends, perhaps even lovers. The Mercedes limo moved soundlessly through the night.

"Arlan told you what we want?"

"Yes," she said. She had a frail, edgy voice.

"And he told you about the reward?"

"Yes."

"Fifty thousand dollars."

Hat and veil nodded.

He was silent for a time. The limo's wheels whirred effortlessly over the pavement. Wind whistled in the corners of the windows. Finally, he said, "Can you do it?"

At first she said nothing. Then, "I'm willing to try."

"I'm at your mercy."

Beneath the veil came a harsh laugh. "Oh, yes, Dr Candelmas. You're at my mercy. Oh, yes."

After a few moments of silence, the woman began crying again, softly, unobtrusively.

Candelmas shifted his position in the seat and looked out the window. They were nearing the Adler Planetarium now, near the place where Emily had last been sighted.

Perhaps tonight he would see her again; perhaps tonight.

IX

MEREDITH HAD NO IDEA what time it was when the phone woke her. She had taken a sleeping pill and was extremely groggy. Reaching for the phone, she knocked the alarm clock to the floor.

She got the receiver to her ear and said, "Hello?"

She knew instantly that this was her mysterious caller. No words would be said. There would just be the static.

"Hello?" she said again, cursing the caller silently and getting ready to slam the phone down.

But tonight there was a surprise.

The caller whispered, in a soft female voice, "Snowkisses."

And then hung up.

Meredith sat up in bed holding the dead phone. Finally she hung up. She could not get the word out of her head. A very special word it was... 'snowkisses.'

That's what her sister Valerie had always called opening your mouth and letting snow fly in.

For Valerie, it was their own little-girl word, and she'd always solemnly sworn Meredith to complete secrecy. Meredith had never told anyone of the word, and she was sure that Valerie hadn't either.

Yet all these long years later, in the middle of a freezing autumn night, the word was whispered once more down the time lines.

But Valerie was dead—

—wasn't she?

Part Two

1

I

SHE HAD ONCE walked in on a man who stood with his shorts comically down around his knees, masturbating as if it were an Olympic event. She had once cleaned up a bed after a woman had clearly and sadly had a miscarriage in it. And she had once seen two men standing in the bathroom kissing each other.

None of this was remarkable, not to anybody, like her, who had been a cleaning woman in a Holiday Inn for the past three years.

Her name was Jesse and she was something to look at. She had secretly dubbed herself The Patron Saint of the Hung Over because she was always getting hit on by chubby salesmen with pinkie rings and good denture work who found themselves in the morning eager to ravish the motel help, particularly a nice slender blonde like Jesse. She was not infrequently propositioned.

Now she pulled her cart down to 304 and leaned into the door and knocked.

Down the hall, room doors were opening and closing. There was shouting and swearing and hurrying and confusion. The usual morning ritual.

She knocked again. Nothing.

She used her pass key and went inside.

The room was in pretty good shape. One bed was still perfectly made, the other wasn't even much rumpled. She changed the sheets on the latter one and then went into the bathroom and got to work. The bathrooms were the real work, of course, always. And at first it had bothered her. When you thought of all the germs you could pick up from a toilet bowl somebody else had used, it was a pretty dizzying—and more than slightly disgusting—concept.

But there were the matters of food and lodging for herself, and so she soon enough got used to toilet bowls others had dirtied.

She spent twenty minutes in the room altogether. She used Ty-D-Bol, Pledge, and Fantastik. She scrubbed, polished, cleaned, and vacuumed. Somebody had to do it. Then she took a break, getting herself a Diet Pepsi.

She lay back on the made bed and sipped her Pepsi and listened to the morning sounds. More doors slamming. More shouting. More frenzy. Salesmen come to Chicago to feed on the office buildings like worker ants invading.

An image came to her—that of a certain room in Perpetual Light and of herself as a teenager, terrified of the room. And darkness.

When she thought of Perpetual Light these days, she tried to think only pleasant thoughts. Thoughts of her friends Valerie and Ellen, of the bright, hot summers, of the smoky autumns. It had been so peaceful sometimes. But other times...

She finished her Diet Pepsi and then straightened up the bed again and went on to do the next room.

II

BY MORNING, the limousine had to stop for its third fill-up. The driver got out and went down to the end of the macadam and smoked a cigarette while the attendant put gas in the tank.

Candelmas stayed in the back seat with the woman.

Despite the darkened windows, sunlight revealed the woman to be rumpled by now, and her hat perched on her head at an almost comic angle. The veil was still in place. Candelmas had not even had a glimpse of her face. She wouldn't let him.

"Shall we go on?" Candelmas said.

"No."

"But we've accomplished nothing."

"I made no promises, Dr Candelmas. You knew that. And I'm exhausted."

Candelmas sighed. "We have to find her."

The woman sighed. "So you say."

"You know how important this is—to everybody."

"I suppose."

"If you get some sleep today, will you be willing to try again tonight?"

"I'm not sure. I'll have to see how I feel."

The woman sank back in the seat. She said nothing. By the angle of her head, she seemed to be staring out through her veil to the street.

The driver walked back to the limousine and paid off the attendant in cash.

The driver, chewing gum now, got back in the car and started the engine.

Candelmas leaned forward and knocked on the glass separating them. "Take her home," he said.

The driver nodded and put the car in gear. Candelmas allowed his bulk to ease back in the seat.

The woman still said nothing. After a time, the limousine on the Dan Ryan now, Candelmas reached over and took her hand, holding it tenderly.

Beneath her opaque veil, the woman was sobbing softly.

III

AROUND TEN-THIRTY Todd came in and said, "UFOs."

Meredith was finishing a paragraph so she waved at him for silence.

Todd sat on the edge of her desk waiting for her to get done typing. Though she used only two fingers, she was a veritable blur when she really got going. As now.

"There," she said. Then she looked up at him and said, "So you were abducted by UFOs?"

He waved several sheets of Xerox paper at her. "A reader sent these in this morning. Clippings from various Tribs dealing with UFOs in the Chicago area over the last fifty years. She felt it might make an interesting historical piece and so do I."

"She's right. It would."

Todd gave her the sheets. "Nice change of pace from the sober kind of thing we run."

"Afraid we're getting boring?"

"Not at all," he said, "But it won't hurt us to titillate our readers once in a while."

She laughed. "Now there's a cautious word, 'titillate.'"

Todd stood up. He wore what she'd come to regard as his uniform. White button-down shirt and regimental striped tie and preppy tweed jacket and dark trousers with cordovan wing-tips.

He had started to leave her small office when she said, "Oh, Todd, I was wondering if I could ask you a favour."

"Sure."

"Wondered if I could take an extra hour or so for lunch. It's kind of important."

"Of course. Everything all right?"

"Everything's fine."

He stared at her a long moment. "You have one of those faces."

"'One of those faces'?"

"You can tell something's wrong just by looking at you."

"Oh. Great."

He stared at her again. "I just hope it's nothing too serious."

"I'll tell you about it sometime. Probably nothing more than my paranoia."

"You sure?"

"I'm sure. And thanks, Todd. I appreciate it."

He nodded and went back to his office. He looked as if he wanted to ask more questions but had decided to be polite.

The library had microfilm of newspapers dating back to the middle of the past century. It was a familiar place and a familiar process to Meredith, sitting at a machine and watching years, decades, and even centuries roll by on the screen as she sought out this or that story.

This one wasn't so tough to find.

She knew the exact date.

She found it quickly.

THREE STUDENTS AND INSTRUCTOR DIE IN CAR MISHAP. *Three female students and their instructor were killed yesterday when their car skidded off an icy road and plunged straight down into a ravine. Medical Examiner Harvey Fullbright noted that all four passengers were killed when the car hit a dry creek bed below and exploded.*

The rest of the story detailed the efforts required to haul the car back to the road. Three tow trucks had been needed and one of them was itself involved in an accident when it slid off the road and went hurtling down into the ravine.

Because of the charred condition of the bodies, positive identification had been made through dental X-rays.

So all Meredith could do was sit there and stare at the story.

Newspapers didn't make up stories.

Nor did medical examiners falsify findings.

Three students and an instructor had been killed in the car accident. One of the students had been her sister, Valerie, so identified in the story.

Valerie was dead. No doubt about it.

But then who called her last night? Who but Val could possibly know about 'snowkisses'?

"Are you all right?"

"Umm."

"You don't sound very sure."

"Umm."

"In fact, you sound kind of sad."

"I suppose."

"Did you find out something you didn't want to find out?"

"No, I found out just what I knew I'd find out."

"And it still made you sad?"

"Um-hm."

"Mind if I ask why?"

"It would be embarrassing to tell you. Honest."

"Try me."

Meredith looked up at Todd, who leaned against her door frame looking boyish and friendly. In the window behind him, flurries of huge wet snowflakes descended like a tattered curtain over the city.

"On my lunch hour?"

"Right," he said.

"When I took the extra hour?"

"Right."

"I went to the library to look up the story about my sister's car accident."

"Really? Why?"

"That's the weird part."

"What is?"

"I've just had this feeling since last night."

"About your sister?"

"Yes."

"What about her?"

"That she's alive. Somewhere. Somehow."

"Oh."

"I told you it was weird."

"So what did you find out at the library?"

"That she's dead."

"You read the newspaper story?"

"Exactly."

"And you feel better now?"

"I guess. I mean, it's better than having this paranoid feeling that she's alive somehow."

"You want the rest of the afternoon off?"

"God, Todd, I couldn't ask for a sweeter boss."

"You didn't answer my question."

She waved some Xerox copies at him. "While I was at the library, I also checked out some more stories about UFO sightings in our fair city. I plan to sit here the rest of the afternoon and outline my article."

"That was a serious offer. About taking the rest of the day off."

"And that was a serious compliment. About you being so sweet and all."

He laughed. "Why doesn't my wife ever say things like that?" He went back to his office.

IV

THREE BLOCKS from the Holiday Inn where she worked as a maid, there was a small bar with ancient Jefferson Airplane records on the jukebox and a pleasantly shadowy atmosphere ideal for drinking alone. It was a nice place when the lights were off. When they were on, the effect was spoiled somewhat, long strips of black masking tape covering slashes on the booth vinyl, the black and white tiles on the floor looking years past a really good scrubbing. Shadows were nicer; you could hide in shadows.

She usually came here after work and had two, three mixed drinks and spent three or four dollars playing songs from when she'd been a very young girl in the sixties. She even went along with the beefy bartender's fantasy that he was making some progress in putting the move on her.

She was two drinks down when he started in for the day. "So how's it goin', beautiful?"

"Pretty good, Hal."

"You're lookin' great, that's for sure."

"Thanks, I appreciate that."

He pulled out a chair and put his cowboy boot up on it, and leaned forward confidentially. "Guess what I got for next Saturday night?"

"What?"

"Two tickets."

"Tickets?"

He leaned even farther in. "Hulk Hogan."

"What?"

"Not what, who. Hulk Hogan the wrestler."

"Oh. The wrestler."

"The wrestler. Just about the best there is. Except for The Cowboy Killer."

"I guess I don't care for wrestling much."

"You don't?"

"I guess I just never developed a taste for it." She tried to keep any condescension from her voice. Hal was dumb but sweet, and she didn't want to hurt his feelings.

"Oh, I see." But she could tell she'd hurt him anyway, even not meaning to.

And then the door opened.

She could see overcast light fill the doorway and feel cold wind scuttle invisibly across the floor to chill her slender legs, the very same legs that dumb but sweet Hal often complimented her on.

The man appeared in the doorway moments later and she knew right away that she should get up and run. Fast and far.

But the two drinks had made her lethargic and she felt suddenly too old to do anything like get up and run.

The man came inside the bar. He wore a snap-brim fedora and a trench coat. Jose Feliciano was singing *Light My Fire*, a version she actually preferred to The Doors'.

The man stood adjusting his eyes to the darkness and then he came straight across to her. There was something familiar about him.

"Help you?" Hal said. She could tell that Hal, too, had some suspicions about the man. Hal wasn't at all cordial.

"A Pepsi."

"Glass?"

"Please."

All the time he just kept staring down at Jesse, the man did. Never moved his gaze for a moment.

Hal looked at where the man was looking and then he started getting mad.

"It's all right, Hal," Jesse said softly.

"You sure?" Hal asked.

"I'm sure. Really."

Hal glared at the man some more and then he walked back to the door.

Without being asked, the man pulled out a chair and sat down. He didn't take off his hat or coat. He smelled of cold. "You know who I am?"

"Not who you are, maybe. But what you are."

"You might be surprised."

"I'm too old to be surprised."

"You're thirty-seven. That's not too old for anything."

Hal came back with a can of Diet Pepsi and a small glass filled with ice. He set it down in front of the man. He looked at Jesse. Jesse nodded that everything was fine. Hal went away.

"He seems to like you."

"Yes, he does, doesn't he?" she said.

"Candelmas is looking for Emily."

"You came here for a reason, I assume," she said.

105

"There's a man who'd like to talk to you."

"A man?"

"My boss. A man named Bova."

"I've never heard of him."

The sleek, hollow smile again. "Well, he's certainly heard of you. In fact, he's fascinated by you."

She knew, then, why he was here.

"It's a period of my life I'm trying to forget," she said.

"He's a fine and decent man, my boss."

"I still don't want to talk about it."

"Not even if talking about it would help other people?" He paused. "Some people are still hurting from their experiences there."

As he spoke she watched his handsome face closely. Who did he remind her of?

"He wants to talk about Candelmas?"

"Among other people, yes."

She was curious now. Who was Bova? What did he want? The prospect of real excitement had started to appeal to her, too. Bova was obviously important.

"I thought I'd finally closed off that part of my life," she said.

The quick, meaningless smile again. "We'll take good care of you. I promise."

"Well," she said.

He eased a long smooth leather wallet from inside his suit coat. He put a crisp twenty-dollar bill on the table. He nodded to the can of Diet Pepsi. "You have expensive tastes."

"Yes, I do, don't I?"

He walked ahead of her, over to the door, which he held open for her.

"You sure about Saturday night?" Hal said as she walked past.

Dumb sweet Hal. As she came even with him, she leaned across the bar and kissed him softly on the lips. "Yes, I am sure about Saturday night, Hal. Sorry."

In the parking lot, she stood next to a black BMW as the man in the trench coat showed her ID that identified him as a man named Cordair from a government agency. He then handed

106

her a card with an address on it. "See you at nine tomorrow morning." He offered her a ride home, which she declined. She watched him pull away. Why did he look so familiar?

V

THE WOMAN in the grey Volvo and the very black sunglasses turned left into Meredith's driveway and then pulled into a parking lot.

There was something almost depressing about the apartment complex on a cold, overcast day like this one. Even though the place was well kept, it was still a place for people who had no permanence. Folks were always moving in and out. Lives were always being changed, scrambled, sundered, a divorce here, a breakup there, a better job opportunity in the East or the West. When you came right down to it, an apartment house was just like a motel except you stayed a little longer.

She wasn't sure why, but thinking about this bothered her.

She got out of the car and started across the windy expanse of concrete to Meredith's section. Meredith wasn't here. Her car was gone. She probably wouldn't be back for another hour, hour and a half.

A red Mazda came into the parking lot from the north. The driver, a man, checked the woman out thoroughly. She knew she was attractive to men, the tall, slender body, the good long legs, the regal if somehow sad face. Men always looked her over this way, and while it didn't bother her, she felt that the men were really rather foolish. She certainly didn't think of herself as attractive.

The Mazda went down to the far end of the lot and parked. The man got out and started across the concrete to his own section. He was still watching her. He probably thought she was some new woman who'd just moved in, ripe for the picking.

She hurried the rest of the way to Meredith's section and then quickly went up the steeply angled steps.

The building was made of red brick and looked to be in very good condition. She got glimpses of other lives as she climbed the stairs. A living room that was something of a mess, a kitchen

107

that looked tidy and cosy, a bedroom with a black lacy bra tossed carelessly on the bed, a TV room where two very young children in pyjamas sat watching a Road Runner cartoon on the tube. Seeing all these things, she felt a curious emptiness, as if she were something other than human and observing the rituals of a species that was alien to her.

Sometimes the loneliness is the worst price of all.

Those old warning words came back to her as she neared the top of the steps. She felt her heartbeat quicken and knew it wasn't just the exertion from climbing the stairs.

The panic was coming again and she had to deal with it quickly.

She reached Meredith's door on the third floor a few minutes later. She took the small pick from her purse, looked in both directions to see if anybody was watching her, then let herself inside Meredith's apartment.

The door closed behind her, she went to work quickly.

Ten minutes later the woman with the black sunglasses was back in her grey Volvo, pulling away.

VI

GAGE WAS WORKING through his phone messages when Flannagan showed up.

Flannagan made a face at him and sat on the other side of the desk. He was a big blonde man with a face ruddy from drinking and the winds along Chicago streets. He always wore good suits, snappy cuff links, and talked incessantly about his current woman. He'd managed to go through three wives without producing either children or anything resembling a commitment on his part.

Gage said, "No, ma'am, I'm not trying to harass your son. I'm sure you're right, I'm sure he's a good boy but I really need to talk to him about the night Mr Enro at the grocery store was murdered." Pause. "He's not necessarily a suspect, ma'am, but I definitely need to talk to him. Now, I've left you my number and I'd really appreciate it if you'd have him call me when he gets home from work tonight, all right?" Pause. "Thank you very much. I appreciate it."

After Gage hung up, Flannagan grinned and said, "He sounds guilty to me."

"Me, too, actually. That's why I want to talk to him."

Flannagan lighted a Merit. The smoke smelled good to Gage, a recovering former smoker. Too good, dammit, even after all these months. "Tell you somebody else you'll want to talk to."

Gage laughed. "Why do I think you're going to tell me about your latest conquest?"

Flannagan looked genuinely hurt. "You don't want to hear?"

"Sure, I want to hear. Just kidding." Flannagan took his women seriously. For a few months at a time, anyway.

"She's a nurse."

"That can come in handy—"

"Head nurse, actually. Good gig. Lots of bennies."

"Oh, God, Flannagan, you haven't spotted wife number four here, have you?"

"Never can tell, pal. Never can tell."

"And she's gorgeous."

"You bet. Redhead."

"And she's built so well she'll make me weep." That was one of Flannagan's favourite expressions and Gage loved throwing it back at him.

"You can make fun but wait till you see her."

"Those must be wedding bells I hear in the distance."

Flannagan flicked ashes into the wastebasket. "Only one problem."

"Oh?"

"Kid."

"Kid."

"Eight-year-old."

"Ah."

"I mean, I don't have anything against kids but this one's—different."

"How?"

"Reads."

"Reads?"

"You know, sits around the apartment all day and reads.

109

Doesn't like sports. I tried to take him to a Bulls game and guess what?"

"He wouldn't go."

"Exactly."

Gage said, "You've had trouble with kids before, right?"

"Just with little Dora."

"Oh, yeah, that's right."

"And that's because she was always playing that classical music. Jesus."

"That's a problem with kids, Flannagan."

"What's that?"

"They're people."

"Meaning what?"

"Meaning they've got their own standards, their own tastes, and their own preferences."

"You sound like a brochure."

"No, I'm just trying to cut them some slack."

"Well, anyway, Janie—that's the nurse—she's getting kind of sensitive to me always bugging her boy to go to a Bulls game. She says I make it sound like he's not a real boy or something, you know."

"Not all boys like sports."

"Yeah, boys who wind up working in beauty parlours."

"I didn't like sports all that much."

Flannagan grinned. "Yeah, I've always kind of suspected that."

Gage waved a handful of pink phone messages at him. "I know you came up here for a reason." Flannagan worked in the other part of the building. He used to come over whenever he wanted Gage's wife to fix him up with one of her friends. For a few years there, his wife had had an endless supply of good-looking friends. "I know you're working on the Jacob Myles thing."

"Right."

"How's it going?"

"Not at all well."

"I hear whoever did him in really worked over his head."

"You remember that hammer murder on the South Side on

110

Archer a few years ago?"

"Right."

"This was one of those jobs."

Two years ago a husband had come in and found his wife in bed with another man. The husband, who hadn't been feeling well, had come home from work early. He went berserk. He was one of those prototypical men-next-door whom neighbours unfailingly characterised as 'sweet' and 'thoughtful.' Well, he hadn't been sweet and thoughtful this particular day. The doc from the coroner's office said he'd never seen anything like it. The entire skull—the entire cranial region plus the occipital bone on both of them—had not merely been pounded into pieces but had been hammered into tiny bits and even into a fine powder. The doc said the husband must have spent hours pounding the skulls into that condition. Gage, who'd arrived late on the crime scene, had seen the two stiffs just before they'd been zipped up into body bags, and they'd both looked decapitated. There was just nothing left of their heads.

"This Myles," Flannagan said, "he used to teach at some place called Perpetual Light, right?"

And for the first time today Gage was genuinely glad to see Flannagan. Flannagan was going to tell him something useful. Gage could feel it. He was excited and grateful. "That's right, my friend, why?"

"Well, like I said, Janie's a nurse, right?"

"Right."

"Well, yesterday they got this stiff brought in—this old fart named Croft—and she just happened to notice what he'd done most of his life."

"Which was?"

"Which was teach at this place called Perpetual Light."

"How did he die?"

"That's the weird part. They're not sure."

"Huh?"

"True facts. He was in the bathtub and somehow he got scalded. Third-degree burns over most of his body."

"That is strange. But how'd she make the connection to Perpetual Light."

"We were going over the list."

"The list?"

"List of murders for the day. And questionable deaths. The printout."

"You go over it with her?"

"She kind of gets off on it," Flannagan said. "So every night I bring it over to her place and—" He shrugged. "And we just kind of go over it. So anyway, she made the connection."

Gage was still wondering about what kind of person would like to go over a daily computer list of murders.

Flannagan said, "I just thought you'd like to know."

"That's nice of you."

"They're listing it as accidental."

"No suspicion of foul play?"

"None so far."

Flannagan stood up. "Well, I'd better go grab the list and head out to Janie's. She's got this really fancy apartment out near Schaumberg. They've got a small gym there for the tenants and I work out there."

And with that, Flannagan offered a chipper little salute, and went away.

There was something sad about Flannagan. He would never quite be an adult somehow, and Gage always regretted kidding the guy the way he sometimes did.

He turned back to his telephone and picked it up and started ploughing through the messages once again.

But all the time he kept thinking about a man named Croft who'd died mysteriously in his bathtub and who'd spent a good share of his life teaching at Perpetual Light.

That was two teachers from the place dead within a week of each other.

2

I

MEREDITH REACHED HOME twenty minutes later than usual.

There had been a six-car smash-up on the freeway. She'd had to glimpse a woman lying flat on the pavement, blood flooding from some part of her body. Meredith was squeamish about such things. Earlier she'd thought of making herself a hamburger for dinner. Now, the thought of food held little appeal for her.

After parking and getting out of the car, she noticed that Jim Treblinka's red Mazda was moving up toward her in the dusk's shadows, just as the parking lot lights clicked on.

"Hey, babe," he said.

Jim was a twice-divorced insurance salesman who called all women 'babe' and all men 'guy.' For some reason she'd never been able to understand, she sort of liked him. Maybe because he was so much of a loser and seemed oblivious to the fact. There was something endearing to this kind of innocence.

"Hi, Jim."

He looked her over, clearly liking what he saw. "Lookin' good, babe."

"Thanks, Jim. You're lookin' good, too."

He cocked his head a moment and studied her, as if he might just have suspected that she was making fun of him a little. He apparently decided she wasn't. "Big doings tonight, huh?"

"Not that I know of. I was hoping there was a good movie on HBO."

"Catch the one with Redford."

"Good, huh?"

"Fantastic, babe. Really."

"Well, Jim, I'd better be getting upstairs."

"Where's your friend's car?"

"My friend?"

"Sure. Babe in the grey Volvo. Saw her pull up here and then go into your place upstairs."

"What?" She realised how frantic she sounded. She looked around the parking lot at the backs of the buildings, at the neat row of Dumpsters to the right, at the parking slots that were just now beginning to fill up.

"Sure. That's why I asked you about big doings tonight. Just figured when you had some babe visiting you—well, you know that gals like to go out and have a good time just as much as

113

guys."

"A grey Volvo?"

"Yeah. Sure. Hey, you sound kind of upset."

"And she was wearing a head scarf and dark glasses?"

"Right, but—"

"How long ago was she here?"

He shrugged. "Gosh, I'm not sure. Hour and a half, something like that. But what's wrong?"

She realised she must look and sound half crazed. "Just a family squabble."

"Family? You mean you're related to her?"

"Yes," Meredith said, raising her head to look at her apartment. The window was dark, shining faintly with a patina of moonlight. The rectangular picture window seemed ominous now, as did the windows in the other apartments, even the lighted ones. She wanted to get in her car and drive away. She no longer wanted to live here.

"Hey, babe," Jim said. "You want me to come up with you?"

She almost laughed. Jim had been trying to connive his way into her apartment for months. Nothing worked. No matter what reason he came up with, she came up with a better one for keeping him out.

Now he'd just been handed the best excuse in the world.

He wanted to come in to protect her.

"Oh, that's all right."

"Babe, listen, I'm not a bodybuilder or anything like that but I can take care of myself. Trust me."

"It's all right. Honest."

"Could be something wrong up there."

"There could be but there probably isn't."

She was half tempted to take him up on his offer, that was the terrible thing. She absolutely didn't want to walk into that dark apartment alone.

But with Jim along she wouldn't be alone the rest of the night. He'd find some excuse to hang around and then what would happen?

No, it was better to suffer her fate, whatever it was, than

try to get through an evening with a gonadic swinger like Jim.

"You're sweet and I appreciate it," she said, trying to look and sound brave, "but I'll be fine. Truly."

"Up to you, babe."

"Thanks, anyway, Jim."

"Talk at you later."

"Uh-huh," she said. Even caught up in her fear, his cliché grated on her. *Talk at you later*. Right.

Jim's car pulled away. He drove down to the end of the lot, his brake lights flaring like small phosphorescent explosions, and then he quickly turned right. Even from here she could hear his tape deck playing a thunderous rock song. Poor nerdy Jim.

She sighed, straightened her shoulders, and started walking toward her building.

She thought of the time at Perpetual Light when she'd inadvertently been locked out of the main house at night. It took only minutes or so for her to find a way back in, but during that time she'd imagined demons of every sort coming after her. She felt a little like that now.

She started up the stairs, making a small but purposeful fist of her right hand.

Maybe having Jim come along wouldn't have been such a bad idea after all.

In all, it took her five minutes to reach her doorway. There were four other doors on her floor, each along the same entrance walk. She fumbled in her purse for the keys, all the while keeping her eyes on the dark picture window. Was anything moving inside? Who was the woman in the grey Volvo exactly, and what did she want anyway? And what could she possibly be looking for in Meredith's apartment? And one more thing: How could she get inside without a key?

Meredith found her key.

She inserted it carefully in the door lock and turned the knob.

The door opened. She stayed where she was, right on

the threshold, and looked inside.

She could make out the shape of her furniture. In the shadows, it all reminded her of dozing animals.

She could make out the smells of this morning's oatmeal. She could also make out the scent of the room freshener she'd used while cleaning and dusting last night.

She took her first step into the apartment.

Odd, how unfamiliar it all felt, as if it belonged to someone else, and she were nothing more than an intruder.

She was debating whether or not to close the door behind her when the wind decided it for her, slamming the door shut with frightening suddenness.

She felt entombed now, standing in the shifting shadows of the living room, not knowing what to do next.

Once again she thought of Jim and how maybe she should have invited him along, but then she decided no; she was being silly.

She went over and bent down to the table lamp and clipped it on.

Warm yellow light spread softly throughout the room. Everything looked familiar and cosy to her again.

Curiously, nothing looked out of place. From too many TV movies she'd learned what a 'tossed' room looked like. This one didn't look tossed in any way.

She went over to the closet and took her coat off and hung it up. She came back to the centre of the room to look around some more.

Still nothing seemed wrong, not disturbed in the least.

Steeling herself, she decided to examine her apartment room by room.

Why would the woman in the Volvo have come up here anyway?

The kitchen and the back porch checked out fine. Nothing untoward whatsoever. She lingered for a moment on the porch, staring up at the sky and a jet that was leaving cold pink contrails in the purple winter dusk.

Chilled, she went back inside to the bedroom.

Without quite being sure why, she paused before she

116

pushed open the partially closed door. She had an inexplicable sense of *presence* here. Not that somebody was here now, but that somebody had been here.

She opened the door completely and went inside.

Light from the rear parking lot shone through the half-closed drapes. Distantly, she could hear a car door slam below, and then voices buoy up and then sink beneath the wind. For a moment, she was struck by the same sense of unfamiliarity she'd experienced when first coming into the apartment fifteen minutes earlier.

She started across the room to the bed and the lamp on the nightstand.

The phone rang. She went to it and picked it up, clicking on the lamp at the same time.

"Hello."

"Hi. Just wondered how you were doing."

"Somebody was here." Now that the light was on, she surveyed the room. "The woman in the grey Volvo."

"What?"

"One of my neighbours said he saw her come up."

"Are you all right?"

"I'm fine. Just nervous and confused." Her eyes roamed the room. The closet doors were open. She could see that nothing lurked inside. The bureau looked unbothered. And her one luxury, the make-up table, appeared untouched in any way.

"I was calling to see if I could take you out for something to eat," Gage said.

"That's odd."

"What is?"

"I'd been planning on putting on my pyjamas and seeing what was on TV. Spending the night alone."

"Changed your mind?"

"Yes. Now I know why people say they feel violated when somebody burglarises their home."

"You scared?"

"A little bit."

"I can be there in twenty, twenty-five minutes."

"The faster the better, Gage."

"You can always go sit in your car and wait for me."

"I'll be all right. But I'll be glad to see you."

"Won't be long. I promise."

She had just hung up the phone when she noticed the box in the corner. She hadn't noticed it at first because it was a neutral grey colour that got lost against the stern grey fibres of the carpet and the shadow that the lamplight cast in the corner.

The box wasn't hers. Didn't belong to her.

She promptly went to it and bent and started to pick it up, and then had an absurd notion.

What if it were a bomb?

She straightened up, suddenly looking at the box as if it were a coiled snake about to strike.

What if it *were* a bomb?

She stared at it some more. It was a large oblong fashion box such as a dress or a coat would come in. There was no store name on the front, no twine on the sides.

Just a box, she thought, the idea that it contained a bomb fading now.

She bent over and lifted the box up—it was very light, she even wondered for a moment if it might not be empty— and then she set it on the bed in the glow of the lamp.

She sat next to the box and stared at it some more.

Obviously, this was what the woman in the grey Volvo had left. But why? What was in it?

Almost without thinking, she carefully removed the lid from the box and peered inside.

Her eyes filled at once with tears.

She looked at a pink cashmere long-sleeved sweater that had been folded neatly in the box. Dark blotches discoloured the cashmere. She knew exactly what they were, exactly what the sweater was.

Valerie had been wearing it the day she died in the car accident.

The blotches were blood. Dried blood. Val's blood.

She lifted the sweater reverently from the box and laid it

out neatly on the bed. Dr Candelmas gave each child at the orphanage one nice gift each Christmas. He had given Val this sweater. It had been Val's pride, almost beyond reason. She'd seemed to glow whenever she wore it.

Meredith's attention returned to the box.

All that remained was a white number-ten business envelope.

She picked it up, hurried to open it.

Inside was a single photograph. The identity of the woman was obvious. The head scarf. The dark glasses. This was the woman in the Volvo.

She held the photo for a long time and stared at it.

Who was she?

The sound of the phone startled her. She gave a little gasp and then stretched across the bed and picked it up.

"Hello."

"Babe?"

Oh, God.

"Babe, listen, this is Jim."

"Hi, Jim."

"I got to the bar here and ordered myself a toddy, but before I could drink it I decided I had to call and see how you were doing. You know what I mean, babe, how could I have a good time when one of my best friends was playing woman-in-jeopardy?"

She almost laughed. He was so silly, yet so innocently sweet, too.

"I'm fine," she said.

"You sure? I mean, nobody's holding a gun to your head and making you say that, are they?"

"No gun, Jim. I'm all alone."

"I can always come over."

She wanted to say it gently, so as not to hurt his feelings. "No, Jim, I'm fine, honest."

"Okay, babe. Before I made a night of it, I just wanted to check in."

"I appreciate it. I really do."

If he'd been here now, she would have given him a kiss.

119

The sort of kiss you give a nerdy younger brother.

"Well, babe, *ciao*," he said.

"Thanks again, Jim."

She left the box and its contents on the bed and went into the bathroom. She didn't have long to get ready for Gage.

She kept trying not to think about the bloodstains on the pink cashmere sweater.

She wanted suddenly to be out of the apartment, in the chill, reassuring air of the dusk.

In the bathroom, she hurried with her washing and her make-up, and hurried, too, with the freshly laundered skirt and blouse she put on in the bedroom. She tried not to glance at the bed and the box that lay on it.

Done dressing, she clipped out the bedroom light. In moments, she was in the living room.

She had just started thinking about the sweater again when she heard the knock on the door.

"Meredith! Open up! It's me, Gage!"

She crossed the room and opened the door. Before she could say anything, Gage took her in his arms and held her tenderly.

II

BY THE TIME they reached the restaurant, Meredith had told Gage nearly everything.

His first response was "I don't think I know enough about Perpetual Light."

"Why?"

"That's what ties all these things together."

"Perpetual Light?"

"Sure. Three people are killed, they all work at Perpetual Light. A sweater is returned to you that belonged to your sister—she lived at Perpetual Light."

They were just pulling into the restaurant parking lot. People bent into the wind and hurried toward the warmly lighted windows.

Meredith said, "There's a chance she's alive."

He kept his eyes straight ahead, pulling the car into a space.

"Do I sound crazy?"

"No."

"How come you won't look at me?"

He looked at her. "I don't want to see you get hurt."

"Meaning?"

"Meaning I don't want to see you get your hopes up."

"She could be alive," Meredith said.

"She could, yes."

"How else can you explain the sweater?" Meredith said.

"I can't."

"But you still don't think she's alive?"

"There are other possibilities."

"Such as?"

She realised how angry she sounded. She couldn't help it.

He reached over and took her hand gently in his. "Have you ever read any articles on digestion?"

"Not that I remember."

"Well, all of them make the same point."

"And that is?"

"That is that you should be relaxed before you eat."

"She could be alive."

"I know."

"I don't want to start crying."

He reached over and kissed her on the forehead.

"I want her to be alive."

"I want her to be alive, too," Gage said.

"You do?"

"Yes. For your sake, Meredith."

"I never had a chance to say good-bye to her."

Gage looked at her and smiled. "Maybe you'll get your chance, after all."

Gage got out and went around and held the door for her. Five minutes later they sat in a cosy booth, drinking coffee and waiting for their dinners to arrive.

3

AROUND NINE the next morning, snow flurries began again, flickering down from the slate-grey sky like the last pieces of confetti from a party suddenly turned sullen.

The office complex out near Burnham Park looked impervious to whatever the weather had to offer. Wide, squat, the brick buildings resembled bunkers that had been designed with a few minor concessions to architectural fashion—hence the pseudo-Georgian flourishes, hence the curiously hipped roofs.

Inside the largest building, on the second floor, in Room 208, Jesse sat in a long, bare place dunking an orange-frosted doughnut into a cup of black coffee. A handsome white-haired man who looked like a TV senator pointed to a movie screen that fed down from somewhere in the ceiling. The man's name was Bova and he used a long, official-looking pointer to tap the screen every so often.

"You were there how long?" Bova asked. He had earlier explained that the government was looking into several groups that had experimented with children in the fifties, sixties, and seventies. They did follow-ups on the students to see if any special powers had been developed, and checked into the people who'd run the experimental schools to see if any laws had been broken.

Jesse swallowed part of her doughnut and said, "Seven years."

"In Building A?"

"In the main building, yes."

"We call it Building A."

"Building A, then. Yes."

"Were you ever on the fourth floor?"

"Yes."

She dunked the last fourth of her doughnut. She needed the quick bright energy of sugar. She was tired. Even a little burst of energy, sugar energy, would be nice.

"What went on on the fourth floor?"

"Special classes."

"What kind of special classes?"

"The more gifted students were given difficult problems to solve with telepathy."

"What kind of problems?"

"We'd be put in pairs. One person would be the sender and the other person the reader. I was always afraid to be the reader."

"Why?"

"I was afraid I wouldn't be very telepathic and that I wouldn't be able to read the sender's message."

"What happened if you couldn't read the message?"

"Usually, we'd just switch roles."

"Did you enjoy being the sender?"

"Yes." She smiled. "Once there was a boy I had a crush on. He was my partner one day. He had very strong talents. Anyway, he read my thoughts and learned that I had this crush on him. It embarrassed both of us."

"So you had fun?"

"Sometimes."

"Was it ever not fun?"

"Oh, sure. Most of the time it was hard work. Plus, for people our age, it was also boring."

"I have a new slide I'd like to put up on the screen."

"Fine."

"You're ready?"

"Ready."

She waited.

Bova walked over to the table and picked up a remote slide-changer. He clicked it a few times.

She watched the screen.

Bova went through several black slides. The noise of the rotating carousel was enormous in the big empty room.

When she saw the slide, she made a sound very much like a cry she was trying to suppress.

"You're familiar with this?"

"Yes." She could barely talk.

"I want to ask you questions about it."

"No."

"No?"

"I won't answer them."

"Why not?"

"I don't want to talk about it. Or think about it." She got up from the table and looked wildly about the room. She wanted to escape. She did not want to sit here and look at this slide and talk about it.

She started running.

Her flats made slapping sounds against the wooden floor. She was headed to the back of the room. Bova was too old and slow to catch her.

She would escape.

She reached the rear door and put her hand on the knob.

The rear door was jerked open and there stood Cordair, looking as sleek and pious as ever. She froze.

"We really need your help on this, Jesse," he said in his reasonable midwestern way. "Now, why don't we go back and sit down?"

You son of a bitch, she thought. You rotten son of a bitch. She grudgingly went back and sat down.

II

DURING HER LUNCH HOUR, Meredith went back to the library.

On a rainy late autumn day such as this, she wanted to go find a good novel and sit in one of the reading rooms and let the rain slide down the window. People would come in and out with bright yellow umbrellas and flick silver raindrops from their hats. There would be something snug and cosy about it, something of an ideal girlhood she never quite had. Of course, it was just a daydream.

She went immediately to the viewers and the microfilm.

She knew just what she was looking for this time.

Instead of just one newspaper, she found four. Four would certainly offer more information than just the one had.

124

She had come armed with quarters, and over the next forty-five minutes she almost continuously rolled coins down the metal throat of the reproduction machine.

By the time she was ready to leave, she had rolled twenty-one sheets of paper together. She tucked them under her arm, unfurled her umbrella, and marched back out into the cold, wet day.

She was halfway to the parking lot when she saw the grey Volvo. It sat three rows back from Meredith's car. It was too far away to get a good glimpse of the woman, but even from here Meredith could see the shape of a human head and a headscarf and dark glasses.

Meredith went over to her car, unlocked it, and dumped the pages on the front seat.

She closed the door again, not locking it this time, and started walking quickly to the back of the lot.

It took a while for the woman in the Volvo to figure out what Meredith was doing.

Meredith got almost halfway there before the woman realised that the person she was stalking was suddenly stalking her.

Meredith started running toward the Volvo.

The woman, in panic, ground the gears as she backed out of her parking space and wheeled around so she could exit the lot quickly.

But Meredith kept running.

She almost managed to catch the Volvo, too.

Just as the grey car was turning right, toward the rear of the lot, Meredith came even with it and reached out for one of its door handles.

The driver gunned the car.

The Volvo shot ahead.

Meredith was flung against a parked Chevrolet van.

By now, the Volvo was at the rear exit. The woman was hastily paying her parking ticket. The wooden exit arm lifted and the grey car passed through to the other side.

The Volvo disappeared into the steady stream of noontime traffic.

Meredith, soaked, went back to her car and back to her

office.

THE GREY VOLVO was a rental owned by the Midlothian Leasing Company, which was in turn owned by one of the larger Chicago banks, one of the few that hadn't been badly damaged by heavy loans to third world countries. The bank was doing quite well, thank you.

Gage had learned about the Volvo from a computer printout supplied by the licence bureau. He'd written down the number when the woman had been following him last night.

Now he picked up his phone, gulping the last of a ham on rye as he did so, nodded to a detective from another precinct he hadn't seen in a long time, and dialled the number of the leasing company.

A man answered and he wasn't much help. Gage got the feeling that the man didn't want to be much help. Gage asked patiently if he might speak with someone who might be a little more "helpful." That was the word he used, and the man of course saw it as the putdown it was and huffily put Gage on hold.

The next voice was sleek and female. Gage explained that he was a homicide detective and that he was trying to learn some things about a grey Volvo that was owned by Midlothian. "That shouldn't be any problem," the woman said.

So Gage gave her all the pertinent information and the woman said excuse her, please, that she'd be back on the line just as soon as she could. Very, very smooth.

Gage sat there for two and a half minutes finishing off his Diet Coke and listening to the various little dramas being played out in the detective bureau. There was an Italian woman sobbing, a black man pointing an accusing finger at a detective, a detective pointing an accusing finger at a pale white man who looked like a recruiting poster for computer nerds, and there was the captain himself looking resplendent and vainglorious in his uniform as an ageing hippie from the *Tribune* snapped his photo. The *Trib* was doing an article on the Chicago Police Department. The captain had somehow managed to get himself chosen as one of the subjects.

The woman said, "Grey Volvo."

"Right."

"Leased twenty-six days ago to a man named Connard."

"A man? You're sure?"

"Gregory Connard. Gregory is never a woman's name, is it?"

"I guess not. Do you have an address?"

She gave him the address.

"How long is it being rented for?"

"According to this, a month."

" I see."

"Is this man in trouble?"

"Not that I know of."

"You did say you were a homicide detective?"

"Right. But he isn't a suspect."

"Oh?" She sounded disappointed. She'd lost some of her sleekness.

"No. We think he might be an eyewitness, though."

"Oh." She sounded happy again.

"Well, thank you."

"You're welcome."

Gage tore the address of Gregory Connard from his notepad and left the station house.

Gregory Connard lived in a terrible section on the edge of the South Side. If he couldn't afford to live any place better than this, how could he afford to rent a Volvo?

IV

"GREGORY CONNARD."

"Say again."

"Gregory Connard."

"That's his name?"

"Yes."

"C-o-n-n-a-r-d?"

"Yes."

"Gregory?"

"Right."

127

"Why did you become so upset when we showed you his slide?"

"You know."

"No," Bova said, "I don't know. That's why I'm asking you."

"He was the one," Jesse said.

"He was the one who what?"

Jesse sighed. She'd been through lunch, which they'd brought in from Wendy's, and she'd been through a snack, which was a doughnut and more coffee from a snack cart. Now she was drinking a Diet Pepsi. Also, a few hours ago, she'd slid back to her old habit of biting her nails. She really got vicious. They were torn, bloody stubs by now. They hurt. She wished she had Band-Aids for them. She wished her head didn't hurt. She wished she were somewhere else. She wished she weren't Jesse at all and then she wouldn't have to wish the other things.

Rain had made the big empty room damp and it smelled mildewed or something now. It was like a cell.

No windows. The doors never opened. Just Bova's voice constantly.

Thinking of these things, her right hand started to her mouth. She was ready to bite her nails again. But fortunately she caught herself in time.

"He was the one who did what, Jesse?" Bova repeated.

"He was the one who put me in that room that time."

"What room?"

"In the basement."

"At Perpetual Light?"

"Yes."

"Gregory Connard was a psychologist there?"

"Yes."

"Tell me about the room."

She sighed. "I was raped."

"Say again."

"I was raped."

"By Gregory Connard?"

"Yes."

"Tell me about it."

"I don't want to."

128

"Why make it difficult for us, Jesse?"

She looked down at her gnawed nails. Bova was right. What was the use of resisting. "Gregory Connard told me that we needed a counselling session."

"Did he say why?"

"Yes. He said orphans had a lot of special adjustment problems."

"Had you ever seen Connard professionally before?"

"No. But I'd been getting in some trouble at school, so I wasn't surprised."

"What kind of trouble?"

She sighed. "I —I just wanted to get out of there. Perpetual Light was my whole life. I was bored."

"So you went with Dr Connard to the basement?"

"Yes."

"Tell me about the basement."

"I can't."

"You can't?"

"Not really. We took an elevator down—this was the only way you could reach it—and we came out into this little corridor and Dr Connard took me into this room right across from the elevator. So I didn't see anything in the basement except the room I was in."

"What was that like?"

"Just an office, really... nothing special... lots of bookcases and books. There was a large desk and then an easy chair that I sat in and a couch, which was really more like a daybed. It didn't have a back or anything."

"So you had a counselling session?"

"Yes. He asked why I thought I was getting in so much trouble lately and he asked me if I didn't like being at Perpetual Light anymore and he asked me if I knew what antidepressants were."

"Did you?"

"No."

"Did he want to give you one?"

"Yes. He did give me one, in fact, right there in his office. But it wasn't an antidepressant."

"No?"

"Uh-uh. Because just a few minutes after I took it, I started getting very drowsy. I mean, I was so tired, I started sliding down in the chair. I just couldn't sit up straight. I remember a sensation of panic—I mean, all of a sudden I realised that Dr Connard, who I'd really trusted up to that point, had given me something that was going to make me unconscious. He hadn't given me an antidepressant at all."

"Then what?"

"I tried to stand up and get away. I can remember that I didn't even have the strength to even scream properly. I tried but I couldn't."

"What was Dr Connard doing?"

"He was leading me over to the couch. I kept trying to push him away but again I didn't have the strength. He led me over to the couch and got me to lie down and then he gave me a shot."

"A shot?"

"An injection. A needle."

"I see."

"That made me even groggier."

"You were unconscious then?"

"Almost. But not completely. I can just barely remember that he started undressing me. He had some trouble with my panty hose, I remember. He stripped me completely. And he started feeling me—down there. His hands were very cold."

She started crying.

"I'm sorry to put you through this, Jesse," Bova said.

She nodded. She kept on crying.

After a long time Bova said, "Did he rape you then?"

"No. At some point Dr Connard left and turned the lights out behind him. I remember that much."

"And then what happened?"

"For a long, long time I just kind of dozed off in the dark room. I remember having goose bumps and my mouth being very dry and I hurt down there where Dr Connard had used his fingers, because he'd been very rough. And then he came back in."

"What happened?"

"I just remember that he breathed heavily, the way you do when you're stuffed up sometimes. And then—this all kind of runs together—I remember him getting inside me with his penis."

"You know it was his penis?"

"Yes."

"You're sure?"

"Yes."

"Not his finger?"

"No. His penis."

"In the dark?"

"Yes."

"And he said nothing?"

"Nothing at all."

"And then what?"

"Then he was gone."

"Gone?"

"He—ejaculated inside me and pulled out. And then he left the room. I remember the door closing behind him. I lay there and started crying. It was very confusing. I still hurt from where Dr Connard had used his fingers on me. And when I felt myself down there. He'd come inside me. And right away I knew I was pregnant."

"And did you prove to be pregnant?"

"Oh, yes. I started morning sickness not too long after. It was a very rough pregnancy. What I can remember of it anyway."

"What you can remember?"

"Right. Shortly after that I was in the hospital and I don't really recall much at all. The foetus died."

Bova clicked the image of Gregory Connard from the screen. By now, Jesse was crying. Softly.

V

AFTER WORK, Meredith went straight home, drew the drapes, and sat in the centre of the living room floor with copies of the newspaper stories spread out before her.

131

She went through each piece carefully, taking notes on a spiral notepad as she did so.

In one story, she found the names of the girls who died in the accident and wrote them down: Valerie Sawyer, Angela Rosselli, and Wendy Skylar. The name of the teacher who had been driving was Fred Kerry.

In another story she noted that the bodies of the three girls had been taken to Kobler Mortuary near Perpetual Light. She went to the phone book and checked to see if the mortuary was still there. It was.

A final story detailed the county medical examiner's conjecture that the girls had died instantly in the crash. The medical examiner's name was Harvey Fullbright, M.D. She again went through the phone book. She found him in the same town where Perpetual Light had been built. She went back and reread the story and saw that while the story listed him as 'county' medical examiner, it didn't list him as Cook County medical examiner, which she found odd.

Finally, she went back to another story and learned that there was an eyewitness to the accident but that he was mentioned only once and in only one of the stories. His name was Herb Carlson and he farmed near Perpetual Light. Why was he mentioned in only one story? Why wasn't he cited in the wrap-up stories the next day? Had he changed his mind? Changed his story? Again she went to the phone book and looked up a Herb Carlson in the rural-route numbers. All she found was a Herb Carlson, Jr. She noted the name and address on her pad.

Finished here, she went into the bedroom and took the box from the bureau and set it on the bed. She sat down and stared at it. She had no doubt that this had belonged to Valerie. No doubt at all.

Next, she picked up the envelope and took out the photo.

The woman in the grey Volvo with her omnipresent dark glasses.

Meredith wondered again who she was. She'd come close to finding out this afternoon in the library parking lot. If only she'd been a little quicker...

Meredith lay back on the bed, tired from her long day. Todd was planning to promote her to associate publisher next year and he'd spent all afternoon walking her through the vagaries of publishing expenses. The weight and brilliance of paper, and the cost of that paper. Enamelled stock versus non-enamelled stock for the cover. How the computer mailing list was maintained and how to handle subscriber complaints. And so on. She'd taken careful notes, but he'd thrown so much at her that she wasn't sure she'd comprehended it all. She'd have to review her notes and ask Todd to walk her through key sections again.

She fell asleep.

She wanted to get up and take her skirt and sweater off so they wouldn't get wrinkled; and she wanted to get up and turn up the heat a few degrees; and she wanted to get up and wash the day from her face and hands.

But she was too tired.

She simply fell fast asleep.

She wasn't sure when she started seeing the images.

Val was running down a long corridor. She was trying to scream but something kept her from screaming. And then a man appeared carrying a very long hypodermic needle. It was Dr Connard. His strides were getting wider now and soon enough he grabbed Val by the shoulder and spun her around and pushed her up against the wall. He gave her the injection. Right through her skirt, right in the hip. Her mouth made a small round O of pain but still no sound came from her. And then she collapsed in Dr Connard's arms.

When she came awake, she knew that the images of Val had been something other than a dream. They'd lacked the soft, shifting textures of a dream. They were more like images that had been projected directly on her mind somehow.

She went into the bathroom and washed her face and hands. She slipped out of her sweater and skirt and put on a denim blouse and jeans.

She went back to the living room.

She was trembling. She tried to tell herself she was not trembling, she tried to tell herself that she was not disturbed, but denial was useless.

Something about those images of Val…

She went over to the closed curtains and parted them gently for a quick peek at the parking lot below.

The woman in the sunglasses sat in her grey Volvo.

Without quite knowing how, Meredith knew that the woman in the Volvo had something to do with the images of Val.

The phone rang.

Meredith stared at it for three rings before crossing the room to pick it up.

"Hello."

"Your sister didn't die in that car accident." It was a woman's voice.

"Why are you following me?"

"It's time you learned the truth."

"Then tell me the truth. I want to know."

"There isn't time right now. I'll call you later tonight."

Meredith was talking to the woman in the grey Volvo. About that she had no doubt.

But when she took the phone over to the window and parted the curtains to look down at the Volvo, she expected to see the woman with a cellular phone pressed to the side of her head.

But the woman had no phone.

Nor were her lips moving.

She was simply looking straight ahead, her eyes hidden behind the dark glasses.

"I'll call you later tonight," the woman said.

There was a click on the other end of the connection, as if the woman had been using the phone.

But she hadn't.

Meredith slowly lowered the receiver back on its cradle.

This was crazy, impossible.

When the phone rang this time, it startled her.

She snatched it up immediately. "Hello!"

"Hi." It was Gage.

Her voice was shaky and she knew it. "God, am I glad to hear from you."

"Are you all right?"

134

"I'll tell you about it later."

"You sure you don't want to tell me now?"

She hesitated a moment and said, "No. Later will be better. How are you?"

"Overworked but fortunately I love what I do." He paused. "I may have a lead on our grey Volvo."

"Really?"

"A man named Connard."

"Connard?"

"You know the name?"

Now she really wanted to tell him about the dream and the strange call afterward, but all she said was, "There was a counsellor at Perpetual Light named Connard."

"This really gets stranger and stranger."

"How did you find out about him?"

He told her about the car rental. "I'm going over there now. I thought maybe you'd like to ride along."

"Is that legal?"

"Worrywart. I'm off duty so I'm just taking a friend along. Anyway, I'd really like to see you."

"Me, too."

"I can be there in twenty minutes."

"Fine. I look forward to it."

There were no more calls before Gage got there.

VI

YOGI BEAR was running away from the Ranger when George Chesmore noticed that his eyes had started bleeding.

Yogi was one of the cartoons George Chesmore really enjoyed. Yogi reruns were on cable every day at this time and George liked to sit in the rec room and watch him. With Yogi on, George didn't feel he was in a mental hospital. It was easy to pretend he was in a hotel of some kind. Just sitting in his robe and pyjamas and lounging. The rec room even had various kinds of pop and candy machines, so when he felt the urge—Dr Birnbaum was always warning him about his excess weight— he took a handful of change over to the machines and really lived it up, the way a man who'd worked hard all his life should.

So Yogi was getting away from the Ranger and just then George Chesmore's eyes started bleeding.

Did eyes bleed?

George thought a long moment but couldn't remember ever hearing of such a thing.

He couldn't see it as yet but he could feel it—hot and sticky, it was—and when he pulled his hand away from his face he could see that his palm was covered with blood.

What the hell was going on here?

This was one of the few times George wished he weren't alone in the rec room. Everybody else was off at supper, leaving George in peace. Everybody except him in this place was nuts. Clinically nuts. He was sure of it.

But it would be nice if that old biddy Mrs Hartman were here for just a few minutes. She'd spent her life working as a nurse and she could probably tell him in a few seconds what was wrong with him. And it likely would turn out to be nothing. Mrs Evans had found a lump on her shoulder one morning and she'd gotten scared and told everybody that she had cancer— see, you can see it right there, that lump, yes, right there. Mrs Hartman had leaned over and peered at it and made a sour face as if Mrs Evans were one silly cluck indeed and said with great disdain, "That isn't cancer. That's a fat tumour. Lots of people have those and they're nothing."

He wished Mrs Hartman were here now. So she could explain.

And that was when the blood started shooting from his right ear.

Shooting, that was the only word for it. Like a goddamned geyser. Like somebody had goddamned struck oil or something.

He just started to scream when he realised what was happening to him. Holy-fucking-shit, George Chesmore thought; holy-fucking-shit.

The night nurse was named Crenna. There had been a time when she'd been at least a modest beauty, but no more. Eighteen years in cuckoo land—not to mention two failed marriages and four noisy kids—had taken both her looks and all the Christian charity the nuns had infused in her… "Remember, girls, when your husband wants sex, it's your duty to give him sex, otherwise he may start suffering from a roving eye and God will hold you, not your husband, responsible." Where the hell had Gloria Steinem been when *Crenna* had needed her?

Crenna was in charge when Mr Newton came waddling down the dark corridor to the illuminated nurses' station.

"He's on the roof," he said, "and he's going to jump."

Crenna's head shot up from the charts she'd been perusing and she said, "What?"

"He's on the roof and he's going to jump." Mr Newton was always heavily sedated—otherwise he was trying to push his unwanted hand down the panties of all the ladies—and for him to reflect this much excitement must mean that something truly horrible must be taking place. Mr Newton, just to complete the picture of keeping himself desirable at all times, slobbered when he spoke.

"Mr Newton, slow down and tell me *who* is on the roof."

She was already getting her slender little legs prepared to start running ass-over-appetite, and preparing her right index finger to hit the red emergency button that sat on a small raised silver platform next to the telephone.

"He is."

"Who the hell is *he*, Mr Newton?"

Apparently Mr Newton had never heard a nurse swear before, because he looked shocked.

"Why, George, of course."

"George Chesmore?"

Mr Newton nodded.

"My God," she said.

And hit the emergency button. And snatched the receiver up from its cradle.

"He's going to jump."

"My God," she said again.

"He was bleeding from his eyes and crying."

Rubber-soled footsteps were already slapping against the polished tiles of the floor as they headed toward the nurses' station.

As Crenna summoned more and more people, she paused to wonder: How could a patient possibly escape from a ward as security-heavy as this one? All doors locked both inside and out and there were alarms and fail-safe systems everywhere. Everywhere. How the hell had Chesmore managed to do it?

"What's wrong?" said Blinkins, the intern. He was out of breath from running.

"Chesmore's on the roof and he's going to jump."

"Jump?" said Blinkins, looking and sounding more like an intern than ever. "Jump off the roof?"

"Yes, Blinkins," Crenna said, "Jump off the roof."

He couldn't see, Chesmore couldn't.

Blood was seeping from both eyes now, totally blinding him. Mostly he could just *feel*. The wind was cold, even rough, on his soft old-man's skin; and the misty dusk was wet in his hair, like quick slimy lice; and cold air was racing up the legs of his pyjamas and freezing his gnarled old testicles into the size and texture of walnuts.

He was right on the edge of the roof.

He was seven floors up.

He was going to make some goddamned mess of himself all right.

Below him now, he could hear voices shouting up at him.

"Chesmore! Chesmore! Go back! Go back!"

And behind him, he could hear footsteps pounding up the stairs and then strong hands throwing back the roof door and footsteps come slapping across the puddles on the roof.

He couldn't see a frigging thing.

He said, "Can you hear me?"

"Yes, Mr Chesmore, I can hear you."

"Who is it?"

"It's me, Mr Chesmore—Crenna."

"Who else is with you?"

"Just the intern and some hospital personnel."

He felt himself start to slip and below—swimming up

138

through the utter darkness before his eyes—came tiny screams.

"I want everybody to leave the roof," Chesmore said.

"But, Mr Chesmore—"

"You're a good woman, Crenna. I'm sorry I'm making your life difficult. But I mean what I say. I want the roof cleared. Do you understand me?"

"Yes."

"And right now."

"I'll do it right now, Mr Chesmore. I promise."

She did just what she said. She moved about the roof shooing them away like naughty dogs.

By now a police chopper hovered overhead, its whirling blades making all the puddles on the roof shimmer. Its searchlights flashed a beam of stark white light on Mr Chesmore, who was still balanced, like a foolhardy circus performer, on the very edge of the roof.

She stalked over beneath the chopper and started waving up to it, a small, determined woman in her nurse whites, shooing them away much as she had the others.

The cop piloting the craft finally got the idea and pulled up, angling to the right, and flew a fancy half-loop rightward so he was away from the building proper.

Crenna hadn't noticed till now but she was freezing her nice little buns off.

She went back to Mr Chesmore.

She peered over the edge. She was a chicken about heights. A true chicken. Seven stories down, a growing, expectant crowd looked up at the roof and Mr Chesmore. This was the kind of drama a crowd loved. Life and death—within a few moments it would likely be live on local news. This was even better than pro wrestling.

In the distance, the tall downtown buildings formed a ragged skyline, the occasional lighted office a vacant, staring eye.

Crenna rubbed the goose bumps on her arms. "Mr Chesmore?"

"Yes?"

"Why do you want to do this?"

"I don't."

139

She stared at him. It was hard to tell exactly what had happened, but there was a sticky crust over his eyes that appeared to be blood. How it had come to be there she had no idea. The same sticky crust seemed to be on his right ear. It seemed that Mr Chesmore had somehow sprung a leak.

God, it was cold up here.

"Mr Chesmore?"

"Uh-huh?"

"If you don't want to do it, why don't you give me your hand and I'll help you back downstairs."

And right then he looked as if he were going to go over backward. He started windmilling his arms and tilted at about forty-five degrees and he let out a bloodcurdling yelp.

The crowd, as one, gasped.

Firemen were there now, stretching out a tarpaulin for him to fall in.

And then, somehow, he righted himself, drew himself erect again, stood on the very edge of the roof but once more under control.

"Holy shit," he said.

"Mr Chesmore, please give me your hand."

"She won't let me."

"Who won't let you?"

"The woman in my mind."

So there you had it. The woman in his mind. Voices whispering. Commanding people. Many of the people in mental hospitals heard such voices. Sometimes they told you to pick up a rifle and go to the place where you work and kill six or seven of the people who'd made fun of you over the years. Or to climb an Interstate bridge and start firing on the cars zipping beneath. Or, as in the case of a nurse like Crenna, to give patients a little too much of this or not enough of that and poof! The patients would be gone just the way that little voice inside your head told you they would.

Now it was Mr Chesmore's voice whispering to him to throw himself off the roof.

"I like you, Mr Chesmore."

"I like you, too, Crenna."

"No, I mean I really *like* you. Let me tell you a secret, all right?"

"Sure."

God, it was cold up here. The wind. The icy night-time temperature. The darkness.

"I don't like all my patients."

"You don't?"

"Some of them I hate."

"Oh, come on, Crenna, you don't strike me as the type who really hates anybody."

"It's true."

"I know what you're trying to do and I appreciate it."

"I'm not just saying this, Mr Chesmore."

"She isn't going to let go. She's very angry. And maybe she's right. I've done things in my life I shouldn't have."

"The woman in your head?"

He nodded. "I know I sound like every other nutcase up here, Crenna. But I'm not. There really is a woman whispering in my head and she's pretty much got control over all my faculties and—"

And then he went. Just like that.

One moment he was teetering on the edge of the roof and the next he was gone.

No warning. No dramatic attempt to reach out.

Just... gone.

He didn't start screaming at first.

He started about the time Crenna, horrified, splashed through a puddle and got to the edge of the roof and looked down.

Mr Chesmore was falling on his backside, his arms straight out from his sides. And now he was screaming. Really screaming. Crenna had never heard anything like it.

And the firemen gathered below with their tarpaulin to catch him started moving toward his approximate landing site.

When Mr Chesmore hit, there was this long, awful moment of silence before anybody could hear the sound of his body hitting the tarpaulin.

Then it came, this hard final whump.

And then Crenna leaned over a little more for a look at

141

where Mr Chesmore had landed. Right in the centre. Arms still widespread. Unmoving.

A doctor was on Mr Chesmore immediately.

The doctor worked with a frantic air that they had warned him against in med school. The crowd didn't help things. Cops were trying to push them back, but they weren't having much luck. What good was a drama when you didn't know the ending?

Finally, the doctor stood up. He didn't do anything as hokey as shake his head, but Crenna could tell from his body language—even from up here—that Mr Chesmore hadn't made it.

Crenna allowed herself a few stern nurse's tears, standing there shivering and rubbing arms knobby with goose bumps.

The chopper was back, vulgar and noisy and oppressive.

Crenna finally came away from the edge of the roof and started back across the shimmering puddles to the door leading downstairs.

I don't want to jump, Crenna, but I can't help it.

This woman inside my head is—

She was going home tonight and have two stiff belts of Johnnie Walker Red Label (a fifth lasted Crenna six months) and take a sleeping pill and pack it in.

Instead of taking the elevator, she walked the seven flights down. She wanted to allow herself a few more stern nurse's tears.

She wasn't worth much of a damn the rest of the night.

VII

AT SEVEN, they told her she could go home.

She stared at them. Just stared.

"Are you all right, Jesse?" Agent Cordair said.

"You haven't told me anything," Jesse said.

"There's not much to say."

"Then you really expect me to believe your story about doing follow-up on all these experimental schools from the

142

fifties and sixties?"

"That's the truth, Jesse," Cordair said quietly.

The empty conference room was still big and bleak. Up front, Bova leaned against the wall, just to the right of the screen, staring at her. Saying nothing. Absolutely nothing.

"How about you, Bova?" Jesse said. "Are you telling me the truth?"

"The truth so far as I know it, Jesse."

"I don't like you, Mr Bova, and I want you to know that."

"I'm sorry you feel that way, Jesse. I'm just a man doing his job."

Jesse looked at Cordair. "You know that some of them are still alive. The gifted ones. They're the ones you're after. You've got your own plans for them."

"I'm afraid I don't know what you're talking about."

She looked at him and shook her head, as if he were among the most pitiful creatures on this planet.

She stood up and put on her cheap bright raincoat and picked up her cheap bright umbrella and slid into her cheap black flats. She could never remember a time when she'd felt more isolated.

Jesse turned, and started for the front door. At the sound of his voice, she looked back.

"I'll give you a ride home."

"I'll take a cab."

"You don't have much money."

"I'll still take a cab. I don't want anywhere near you anymore, Cordair."

"I wish you didn't feel this way, Jesse."

"They're alive somewhere, a few of them are, and you won't tell me where."

From the front of the room, Bova said, "You seem to be confusing our roles here, Jesse."

"And that means what, exactly?"

"We feel they're alive—there's some evidence that they're still alive—but we don't know where they are. We thought that you did perhaps."

And with that, a harsh laugh escaped her. "You think I

know where they are? My God, if I did, don't you think I'd be with them?"

She stared at Cordair some more and left.

Rain on the back window of the cab lent the passing streets the feel of a watercolour painting, the red and blue and yellow and green of neon bright and gauzy.

The driver, thankfully, didn't talk much.

She sat tight in the corner of the back seat feeling tiny and old and scared. She forgot that she was an attractive woman or that she had a laugh that gave others the pleasure of sunshine or that she had a good, quick mind.

At the moment, she thought of none of this.

She thought only: they're alive somewhere... hiding... Waiting, perhaps.

The cabbie said, "This kerb all right?"

"Fine."

She sat forward in her seat and opened her purse and fumbled inside until her fingers felt the wrinkled surface of worn money. She held several bills up to the back window, making sure of the denomination. She tipped him two dollars. Maybe that wasn't enough. Right now she didn't care.

She got out and chunked the door shut. The cabbie took off immediately, leaving her standing on a wind-whipped sidewalk in front of a crumbling old three-storey frame apartment house that had probably been a pisser when Calvin Coolidge was running the country.

She was ten steps up the walk, about to put her right foot on the first step of the front porch, when she felt the subtle shift in her consciousness. It was as if somebody had turned up the volume of a radio. Not a lot. But enough so that she was now hearing things she couldn't hear before.

I'm waiting in your room. Hurry.

My God, Jesse thought, wanting to laugh and cry at the same time. My God.

She hurried up the front steps and inside the apartment house. As always it smelled of dust and furniture polish and Mr

Donnelly's Prince Albert pipe tobacco.

But tonight there was no time to linger.

She hustled across the vestibule to the staircase, taking the steps two at a time. She was quickly out of breath. She didn't care.

Her room was on the third floor.

By the time she reached her door, she had her key in her hand. She fitted it into the lock of 308 neatly and then went inside.

Emily hadn't been lying.

She was in there waiting.

VIII

GREGORY CONNARD lived in a small, dark house that sat on a corner and was half hidden by several tall hedges.

Gage went around the block twice, and up the alley once, but found no sign of a grey Volvo anywhere.

Gregory Connard might be here, but apparently the woman wasn't with him.

Gage parked halfway down the block, shut off the headlights, and turned to Meredith. "You sure you want to do this?"

"Yes." All she could think of now was Valerie and the possibility that she was somewhere, somehow alive. So many years had passed but the pain of Val's loss burned bright again, as did Meredith's prayer that she could see her sister and hug her and laugh with her once more.

Gage was just about to say something else when a dark sedan swept by them. The sedan went down to the end of the block, right in front of Connard's house, and stopped.

"Who's that?" Meredith said.

"I don't know."

"Connard?"

Gage shook his head. "Somehow I don't think so."

They sat in the dark car, watching the sedan. They could make out two silhouettes in the sedan's front seat. Both wore hats. Both had their heads turned to look at Connard's dark house.

The passenger door of the sedan opened.

A big man in an overcoat got out. Briefly, the dome light flashed stroboscopically on the interior of the car, then died when the big man slammed the door shut.

The big man went up to the kerb, stepped up, and started walking briskly toward Connard's house.

"Any idea what he's doing?" Meredith asked.

"No."

Gage shoved his hand inside his sport coat and yanked his police revolver free of its shoulder rigging.

"This could get sticky," he said.,

She couldn't take her eyes off the weapon. It looked outsize. It both fascinated and repelled her.

"I want you to stay here," Gage said.

"You're going up there?"

"Yes."

She sighed. "I'm not afraid to go."

"I know. But I'd appreciate it if you'd stay here."

"All right."

He reached up and popped the dome light bubble from its track. He unscrewed the dome light bulb.

"Be back as soon as possible," he said.

Wind rocked the car when Gage opened the door, wind salted with raindrops.

Gage crouched down so low, he was almost walking on his haunches.

He moved without pause toward the parked sedan ahead.

For a time he seemed to disappear in the shadows cast by the lone, dim streetlight, but suddenly he reappeared and stood up right next to the sedan.

In the wavering streetlight she could see that he had his revolver flush against the driver's window.

Gage said things she couldn't hear and then reached out and pulled the door open.

Once again the dome light flickered as the driver got out of the car. The door slammed shut and the light vanished.

By the time the driver had both feet on the pavement, Gage was pointing the gun directly at the man's face.

The man pushed his hands straight up in the air.

Gage said a few more things, let the man respond, and then waved his gun as the man lowered one hand and reached inside his topcoat. He brought his hand back carrying a wallet, which he handed over to Gage.

Gage looked at it carefully, leaning into the pale streetlight. He handed it back and put his weapon back inside his sport coat.

What was going on? Meredith wondered.

Gage and the other man stood talking when the third man appeared again from behind the hedges.

Another sequence of pantomime followed: Gage and the third man were introduced, the man showed Gage his identification, and Gage and the man shook hands. Then the men got into the car, Gage stood back, and they drove away.

Gage came back to his own car and opened the door and got in.

He smelled of night and cold.

"Who were they?" Meredith asked.

"Government agents named Cordair and Bova."

"They're looking for Connard, too?"

He nodded. "Bova went up and checked everything out. He said he didn't find anybody inside."

"Oh."

And then she felt it; just then. She felt her pulse quicken.

Help me, help me.

Gage leaned forward and started the car. "Not much point in sitting here, I guess."

Help me.

Gage waited while a panel truck passed and then he angled the car away from the kerb.

Help me.

"You're quiet all of a sudden," he said, glancing at her. Then, "Are you all right?"

"I want to go back there," she said softly, just as they reached the end of the next block.

"Back where?"

"To Connard's house."

"Nobody there. The government man already checked it

147

out."

"He's there."

"Who's there?"

"Connard."

"How do you know that?"

"Bova didn't look in the basement."

"Meredith, are you all right?"

He was still driving away from Connard's.

"Please, Gage. Please go back there."

"Meredith, you're starting to scare me."

"I don't mean to."

Gage sighed. "You want me to go back there?"

"Yes."

"Right now?"

"Yes."

"Because he's in the basement?"

"Yes."

"Do you know how crazy this sounds?"

"Yes."

He sighed again. "Are you getting messages from somebody or something?"

Softly, barely a whisper, Meredith said, "That's exactly what I'm getting."

IX

SHE WAS the same woman who had been in Candelmas's limo the other night, Ellen Frazier, helping him to find Emily.

She lay on a cot now, in a dark room. She had been lying down now for nearly two hours.

Candelmas, impatient as always, stood by the window of the motel suite and looked down on the Dan Ryan.

Headlights and taillights were blurs in the cold rain.

"Why don't you sit down?"

"No, thanks."

Dennis Voigt, the driver, sighed. When his boss was nervous, he was nervous. All the driver wanted to do was relax and try to digest the dinner room service had brought over earlier.

"She said she was starting to get images again," the driver said.

"She's been saying that for four nights now. And we still don't know where the girl is. She won't be in Chicago forever. You can bet on that."

Bitterness did not become Candelmas. It made him seem older. He raised his glass of Kentucky mash and sipped.

The driver got up and started hunting through a pile of magazines for something to read. He moved carefully, as quietly as possible. He had been with Candelmas for many years and he knew how the slightest noise could sometimes set his boss off. And then there was always hell to pay.

The woman on the cot in the dark room made a whimpering sound.

Candelmas looked at the driver and then went to the dark door and peered inside. "Ellen?"

He could see, vaguely, a woman's shape writhing on the bed in the shadows. The woman whimpered, then groaned. The sounds carried a certain sexual charge.

"Ellen?" he said again.

Frowning, he turned back to the driver. "Wet a clean hand towel for me and bring it into the room."

The driver snapped to his feet, nodded, and went immediately to the bathroom. Running water could be heard.

In moments, the driver handed Candelmas the damp towel. Candelmas handed the driver his drink. "Thank you, Dennis." He nodded to the dark room. "Needless to say, I don't want any interruptions."

"Of course."

Candelmas nodded again, hefted the towel on his wide, strong hand, and went into the dark room.

He closed the door behind him.

The only light in the room came through the half-slatted blinds. Wet traffic sounds from the Dan Ryan could be heard when Ellen wasn't making her desperate noises.

He went over and sat on the edge of the bed.

Carefully, almost tenderly, he put the hand towel across her forehead. A mere touch of her flesh told him that she was running a serious fever. The towel should help.

He left the towel there a few minutes, holding her damp hand all the while, looking down at her through the shifting shadows of the room, remembering when she'd been a girl at Perpetual Light, so full of innocence and energy and her own odd loveliness. Ellen was no beauty, certainly, but there had always been an essential appeal to her little-girl looks and her easy, genuine smile.

Right now, though, she looked pretty bad.

The headaches had taken their toll—lots of vomiting… lots of sobbing.

"Ellen?"

There was a subtle shift in her breathing pattern. He could tell she was hearing him, at any rate.

He squeezed her hand gently.

"Ellen?"

He leaned closer and kissed her on the cheek.

"Ellen?"

Her eyes opened. She looked confused, even frightened, a moment. Then she recognised Candelmas and relaxed.

"I must really have been out," she said.

"Would you like a drink of water?"

"No, thanks."

"Do you think you could hold food down yet?"

"I'd better not try."

"Then just lie there and relax."

She closed her eyes again.

He waited for what seemed to him a decent interval and then he said, "Have you had any luck?"

"I think so."

He needed to remain calm. "You think so?"

"I kept seeing the same house."

"Is it in Chicago?"

"Yes."

"Did you get any sense of an address?"

She muttered a few things that put him in a certain section of the city. And then she said, "There's a house down the street."

"Did you get an address for that?"

150

"Yes."

And she told him the address.

My God, Candelmas thought. If she could only tell him the street, he could find the house.

He could find the girl.

"Ellen?"

"Yes, Dr Candelmas."

"I need the street address. Can you see a street sign anywhere?"

"No. But…" She paused.

"But what, Ellen?"

"It's by the University."

"You're sure?"

"Yes, Dr Candelmas."

Stay calm. Stay in control. "Ellen?"

"Yes?"

"I need you to go with me."

"In the car?"

"Yes, I'm afraid so."

"But my head and my stomach—"

"I'm sorry to ask you, Ellen, but I need to. If we can drive around the area, I'm sure you can find the right house."

"Maybe, Dr Candelmas, but—"

"But what?"

She looked uneasy, embarrassed. "What if I'm in the car and I have to throw up again?"

He smiled.

She really was such a child.

He leaned over and took the hand towel off and kissed her gently on the forehead.

"Why don't you let me worry about that?" he said softly.

X

HALF A BLOCK away, Gage killed the headlights and coasted up to the kerb.

On the passenger side, Meredith continued to stare at Gregory Connard's small frame house.

151

"He's in there," she said.

Long shadows slipped like playful children across the front yard of the house. No light shone anywhere.

Gage wondered if she was all right. He had seen stress take its toll on even the strongest people. Thinking that her sister might be alive somewhere had seemed to undo Meredith. Now she was talking about cognitive powers Gage wasn't sure existed.

"Why don't I go in and look around?"

"Don't patronise me, Gage."

"I'm not patronising you."

"I know how strange this looks but something's going on. Inside my head, I mean. I can hear him."

"Hear who?"

"Connard."

He sighed. "I see."

She looked over at him. Her voice, in the darkness of the car, was softer now. "No, you don't see, Gage. And neither do I. All I know is that there's a voice in my head and that I believe it belongs to Connard."

He turned to her. "All right, Meredith, I believe you."

"I need to go inside and find out if I'm right."

"I'll go with you."

"You don't have to."

"I want to." He put out his hand and touched her face. "I care about you, Meredith. I mean, that's kind of obvious, isn't it."

"Oh, Gage," she said, and there were tears in her voice, and she leaned over and kissed him tenderly on the mouth. "You're such a good person, Gage. I wish I could help both of us understand this but I can't. All I know is that—the voice—somehow has something to do with my sister."

He squeezed her hand and said, "C'mon, then, let's go inside."

The wind nearly whipped them off the sidewalk, but less than a minute later they were at the back door of the small house and Gage was holding up a small tool that resembled a walnut pick. He put it in the backdoor lock, twisted it around a few times, and then gave the door a heavy push. The door opened. "Strictly speaking." he said. "We should have a search warrant."

He led the way inside.

The stairs leading down were swollen and narrow. Gage clipped on a flashlight. The basement looked ancient, a gas furnace from the 1950s dominating one corner, rows of spindly wooden shelves supporting rows of cobwebbed Mason jars lining another, and several spavined stacks of cardboard boxes completely overwhelming the entire east wall.

Meredith, who suffered from allergies, sneezed several times.

She stood in the centre of the damp floor looking around. Gage watched her carefully. How beautiful she was, even in this strange moment.

And then they heard the moan.

Meredith's head snapped around. Her eyes found the small wooden cell that had once been a coal bin.

She walked over to it, Gage's light splashing yellow across the dry, rotting boards.

The door had only one hinge. It went *scrawww* as Meredith pulled the door back.

Inside, tucked into a corner, was a man. Or what was left of a man. He appeared to have been hacked apart with an axe. One good eye remained in his blood-drenched face. It followed Meredith into the room.

"Connard?" Gage said behind her.

Meredith nodded.

Clearly, she wanted to bury her face in her hands and then flee. But she gulped, and steeled herself, and knelt down next to the dying man in the corner.

"I'm Meredith Sawyer, Mr Connard. I'm looking for my sister, Valerie."

Gage wondered if you ever quit addressing former teachers as 'Mr' and 'Mrs'.

The lone eye stared up at her.

"Valerie? Do you remember her?"

After a time, Connard inclined his head in something resembling a nod.

Meredith glanced back up at Gage. "There's no more mental contact. I'm not hearing anything." Then, "You'd better call an ambulance."

Gage nodded. He stepped out of the room and took out the portable two-way he'd brought along. He kept his voice low. An ambulance was dispatched.

He stepped back into the coal bin.

Meredith was saying, "Why did you say Wyoming, Mr Connard?"

She reached out angrily and took him by his shirt and began to shake him.

Gage heard her curse and sob. "I want to know where my sister is!" she said as she shook him.

Gage knelt down next to her. He put his hands on her wrists and loosened her fingers. Connard slumped back into the corner.

One of his eyes opened again and he spoke. "I did something terribly wrong." Even though his voice was scarcely a whisper, she could hear the shame in his words. "I molested some of the girls at Perpetual Light."

And then he told her what she wanted to hear: that a few weeks ago a young woman named Emily had come here and held him captive and tortured him for his terrible sins. She'd used his rental car—the one he'd been going to take on vacation—to get around Chicago so that she could kill others associated with Perpetual Light. "She hates us and she's been killing us," he said. His eyes closed for a final time.

"He's dead," Gage said softly.

Her hands were covered with Connard's blood as she fell into Gage's embrace. "He said Wyoming," she said. "Something about Wyoming."

She raised her head. "There may be something upstairs. Come on."

In the distance now, they could hear a siren.

Meredith went up the stairs quickly.

The place was much better furnished than might have been expected, with a genuine leather couch and armchairs in the living room, nicely framed Chagall prints throughout the house, and an office next to the bedroom that was neatly appointed and filled with impressive computer equipment.

She started with the desk in the office. She worked with a real frenzy—one teetering on madness, Gage knew—flinging open desk drawers and searching desperately through them.

Finding nothing in the desk, she moved to one of three filing cabinets and started a desperate search through them.

Gage took the other two cabinets.

Just as they heard the ambulance pull up outside, Meredith said, "Wayland."

"What?" Gage said.

"Wayland, Wyoming," she said, waving an envelope at him. "That's where I'm going to find my sister."

Within a minute Meredith was on the phone asking United about flight information.

She still wore her head scarf and dark glasses.

She sat in a straight-backed chair in the kitchen of Jesse's tiny apartment and drank the herbal tea Jesse had made them.

The woman's name was Emily.

"It's nice there," she said.

"I'll bet it is," Jesse said.

Jesse glanced around the kitchen. She'd tried fixing the place up, making it seem more her own, but she'd never quite succeeded. The small gas range and the big white wobbly refrigerator clearly belonged to the landlord. Even the framed photo of Jesse and Valerie standing together long ago in front of Perpetual Light seemed impersonal in this context.

She saw the angle of Emily's glasses and said, "You've never seen that photo before?"

"No."

"It's a pretty good one."

"Yes. It is."

Jesse got up and got them some more tea. In front of the beautifully shaped younger woman, Jesse felt aged, almost slatternly. "That's the funny thing," she said, bringing the cheap dime-store teapot over to their cups.

"What is?"

"My memories of Perpetual Light. They should be dark and

155

terrible and some of them are, of course—but still, we had some pretty good times there. We really did."

"You know I'm insane," Emily said.

"What?"

"I have—seizures. I've killed people. The teachers at Perpetual Light. Now I want to get the rest of you together all at the same time, with my mother Valerie."

Jesse laughed. "Twenty-four hours ago I would have told you to forget it. But now—"

"You'll go with me, then?"

Jesse felt an idiotic grin widen her mouth. The people she'd known at Perpetual Light—the good people anyway—she would soon see again.

"Will Ellen be there?"

Emily shrugged. "Right now she's helping Candelmas try to find me." She smiled. "Maybe we'll all meet in Wyoming."

In her bedroom, Jesse threw open a suitcase and began packing basics. Where they were going, basics would be required.

A few times she felt a curious nostalgia for the shabby little life she'd built for herself here in Chicago. Certainly she wouldn't miss cleaning toilets. Or her angry bosses who saw cleaning women as a step down from slugs. But still, there were things here she liked. WGN radio interviews late at night when she sat in the living room rocker. The feeling of being 'home' at day's end. Some of the neighbours she'd gotten to know.

"There's a car across the street," Emily said.

"Oh?" Jesse said.

"Two men."

"What are they doing?"

"Sitting in their car."

Keeping the light off, Jesse walked across the bedroom to the window. She parted the curtains slightly and peered down at the dark, rainy street.

She recognised the car immediately, and even if the car hadn't been familiar, his posture would have been. Cordair sat absolutely erect, just the way you'd expect a Notre Dame man to sit.

156

"Agents," she said.

"Looking for me," Emily said.

"Yes."

"We don't have long."

"I know."

"Is there a back way?"

"Yes."

"If we get separated, we'll meet at Gate 40 at O'Hare," Emily said.

She came into the room and hugged Jesse.

"We'll be all right," Emily said. "We just need to hurry."

Jesse finished packing, snapped the clasps on the bag.

The two women went into the kitchen.

Jesse nodded to the door. "Down those stairs. They lead to an alley. I'll be right behind you."

"You don't have to do this, you know," Emily said.

"I know," Jesse said. "But I want to."

Emily opened the door and began her quick flight down the steep, slanting steps. Twice she nearly fell.

Jesse was never more than two steps behind her.

They both reached the alley out of breath and frightened. But reaching the alley wasn't the end.

It was only the beginning.

They took off running in the opposite direction from Cordair's dark sedan.

Emily had just entered the alley when a car with darkened headlights pulled from the deep shadows of a garage, blocking her way.

Emily screamed.

But the driver's window came down quickly and a woman inside said, "Get in the car before those agents get you!"

"Who are you?" Emily said, still unable to make out a face.

"Sandra," the woman said. "Mother sent me here to bring you back."

"There!"

Bova was half shouting.

Cordair, however, didn't need instructions.

He had seen Jesse emerge from the darkness of the backyard

into the misty light of the alley.

Cordair wheeled the sedan around, headlights erupting like the eyes of a jungle predator, and started flying across the rain-soaked pavement toward the alley.

The sedan banged and slammed down the narrow alleyway, headlights bouncing up into the fog.

He saw Jesse, who was stumbling as she ran down the alley.

Dumpsters and garage doors and even a stray, startled dog appeared and vanished quickly in the Windshield.

Jesse was now screaming; the men could hear her even through the closed windows.

"Goddammit," Bova said, "You're letting her get away.

Cordair glared at the older man. "Things are under control, Bova. Now, shut up."

Bova glared back. He was not used to a young agent being anything except deferential to him. Certainly, young agents didn't tell him to shut up.

Cordair put the accelerator near the floor.

Now the sedan began to slam up and down on the bumpy bricks with great, almost dislocating violence.

Jesse was at the head of the alley now. She was freeze-framed in a moment of indecision, trying to determine which way to run—right or left.

Jesse's hesitation gave Cordair time to do just what he wanted.

The big car vaulted ahead.

Jesse was trapped. There was no time to run.

The front end of the car caught her just as she started to turn away, lifting her several feet in the air.

The headlights caught her arc through the air and then tracked her body as it flew into a row of garbage cans.

With white bones jutting from her pale flesh, and red blood turning her face into a sleek mask, she lay flat on her back.

Before Bova could say anything, Cordair was out of the car and running to Jesse.

The mind-tap took only moments. She was not dead yet. Cordair was able to find out what he wanted. Wyoming.

Moments later, silhouetted in the headlights behind him,

Bova stood over Cordair and said, "Why are you staring at her that way? Haven't you ever seen a corpse?"

Cordair looked up. A strange smile parted his lips.

"Yes," he said, drawing a small pistol from his jacket, "And I'm about to see another one."

Neat and clean, he shot Bova through the throat, using two shots to make certain the job got done properly. He tucked the gun away.

Then he was in the car, heading for the airport, having just resigned his government post with the two gunshots.

He had joined Bova's group in order to find out exactly how much the government knew about Perpetual Light. Actually, the government knew very little.

Cordair would be safe in carrying out his plans.

Part Three

1

I

TYLER OFTEN JOKED that he wasn't sure the two women were good role models for him. He knew far more about menstruation, leg waxing, and backcombing than was probably good for a red-blooded American teenager.

Actually, he kind of liked the arrangement; or arrangements plural, as they'd moved four times in the past six years.

Tyler was the product of another unholy Perpetual Light alliance: One of the professors had seduced a sixteen-year-old girl. And from the joining came Tyler. The girl, whom the professor was experimenting on with drugs as well as illegal sex ("Jesus Christ, haven't you ever heard of statutory rape?" Candelmas thundered on the day he began to learn what his hirelings had really been doing down the years), became psychotic. So many of them did. While in the steaming shower room one afternoon, she cut her throat with a straight razor, bleeding to death before anybody found her. When Valerie deserted Candelmas, unable to deal with his collapsing empire any longer, she'd grabbed little Tyler (then four years old) and taken him along with her.

Tyler liked being with women fine, these women in particular. Especially after Richard ran away. They proved to be a wonderful combination of mother-sister-friend and—when he managed to catch glimpses of them in the buff from time to time—even girl friend.

True, Tyler dusted, cooked, sewed, and knitted, just as the women had taught him to; but he also fished, hunted, tracked, and watched endless Cubs baseball games.

He considered himself fortunate to have such a relationship with the women.

Especially with Valerie. She might be twenty-five years older than he was, but it made no difference to Tyler. He had a burdensome crush on her and spent a lot of time daydreaming about their future together.

As yet, he hadn't worked up nerve enough to mention any of this to Valerie, of course, but he was certain that he soon would... very soon.

2

I

AS THE LEARJET pushed through the darkness, Candelmas leaned forward to look out of the window. Ellen Frazier had led him to where Emily was staying. He found a letter postmarked from Wyoming. Now he was here himself.

Below, he could see the snow-capped peaks of the Rockies stretching like a jagged belt across the west.

Despite his long life, he had not ever given adequate time to studying all the natural wonders around him. He would go to his grave a very ignorant man, without having experienced even as much as the average tourist. Always, it had been his obsession with paranormal powers; always it had been his dream of a superior human race that would lead mankind to a higher plane of existence.

"Sir."

Candelmas looked up.

His chauffeur, Voigt, stood over him with a bourbon and water on a tray.

Candelmas took it. "Thank you."

"It won't be long now, sir."

"No, it won't, will it?"

"I'm sure we'll find her this time."

Candelmas nodded his thanks.

Voigt went away.

For a time there was just the soft steady whoosh of the jet and rich black night at the window.

Candelmas closed his eyes and put his head back.

Voigt had said that they would soon see the girl, Emily. And they would also see Valerie. Candelmas was sure of it.

II

VALERIE HAD ALWAYS been a strong believer in premonitions and so this afternoon, right after the cold medicine she took to help her sleep, she concentrated hard on the thought she'd had earlier this morning.

I'm going to see Meredith tonight.

She wasn't sure where the thought came from, or what prompted it, or even how it would come true exactly. But somehow she knew it would come to pass.

After putting out the cigarette, rolling over on her side, and saying her usual little-girl Hail Mary, she began thinking about Perpetual Light. Then, for a long time anyway, sleep became impossible.

It was pretty ridiculous when you thought about it, falling in love with Candelmas. He was hardly the sort to charm a young girl. But because of her talents he'd spent dozens of private hours with her. Later, of course, she realised that her fondness for him had more to do with the fact that she'd never had a father figure in her life. She'd been naive… and willing.

Eventually, of course, Candelmas also fell in love with her—though she could see he did so with great reluctance. She'd wanted to tell Meredith of all this, but she knew better—Meredith was too suspicious of the things that went on at Perpetual Light.

Candelmas didn't trust Meredith, and always kept the sisters apart.

The day of the accident, Candelmas saw a way to free Valerie. They would claim that she, along with the others, had died. And then Candelmas could take her away and they could start new lives. The idea of starting over convinced her. She knew she would never see her sister again, but somehow she thought she'd live happily ever after. Candelmas took her to a vast estate up near the Canadian border, where they stayed till heartbroken Meredith went out on her own.

Soon enough, Valerie bore Candelmas three children, Emily, Sandra, and a son named Richard. They returned to Perpetual Light, and the children were tutored exhaustively in paranormal powers.

From clairvoyance to critical ratio; from dowsing to cognitive dream interpretation; from hallucinatory experiences to hypnosis; from psychokinesis to preferential randomness—every aspect of the paranormal as it applied to the individual was pushed, prodded, examined.

Only when Valerie became aware of what was really going on at Perpetual Light did she become afraid. Several scientists were running clandestine experiments with drugs that Candelmas specifically forbade. His own early experiments with these increased paranormal powers, true, but also caused deep and permanent psychosis. There was also circumstantial evidence that pointed to some of the girls being sexually molested by the male scientists.

The scientists were able to hide their experiments when the investigation began. Candelmas felt that perhaps Valerie—whose own paranormal powers had made her prone to hyper-anxiety anyway—was becoming angry because he spent so much time on his work and she wanted more attention. There was also frustration on his part. Not every gifted student had the same powers—some could read minds, some could move objects about, some could cause certain objects to burst into flames, some could, psychically glean the near future. But the gifts were distributed unevenly. And the powers were not reliable. Few students could summon their powers at will, it seemed. The scientists conducting clandestine experiments eventually learned that the 'prime specimen' Candelmas spoke of could not be made a reality without the help of drugs—dangerous drugs, in some cases.

Eventually the renegade scientists even managed to include Candelmas's own children in the experiments. By the time they reached age ten, Emily, Sandra, and Richard were able to move objects at will, set fires, and battle each other with incredible power. Richard even showed the early ability to block Sandra entirely—to deflect her powers with a mental shield, something that made him both superior and frightening as a 'psychic warrior' (a term one of the renegade scientists coined). But on some occasions, Emily proved stronger than either of them.

Even when Candelmas learned what was happening to his children, he didn't side with Valerie, however. He felt that the scientists, while they'd disobeyed him, were ultimately benefiting mankind by helping hone the powers of his children. From the beginning, Candelmas had known that the strongest paranormal powers began to fade when the subject reached his twenties. From then on, only great moments of stress could tap the latent powers. In his children he saw the ultimate hope of Perpetual Light being realised. Someday they would learn how to heal illnesses, how to negotiate truces between enemies, how to help ordinary people realise all their extraordinary potentials.

Candelmas did not seem to notice all the medical and psychological problems his children developed. They were clearly becoming psychotic—given to great rages and dangerous tantrums.

One night Valerie took them away. She had planned for weeks and so when the night came, she had the plane tickets, the two trunks of cash, and the determination.

They lived in San Diego for six years together before Richard, at age sixteen, ran away. She never saw him again but she'd long had the sense that he was still alive and using his powers. Richard had always been determined to be the new species of man his father had so long dreamed of— even though, by everything Valerie could see, the new species was a vengeful, violent breed.

Tyler tried to comfort her, and stayed with her. There were terrible problems, however, with Emily and Sandra. Emily's eyes became blood-filled sacs from time to time; her scalp developed a crusty, blood-seeping covering. All her hair fell out. And she began her travels. She would disappear for two, three weeks at a time. It took Valerie a long time to understand what was going on. And when she knew, she tried to stop it but by then it was too late. Emily was too strong and psychotic for her.

Many times, Valerie had wanted to call Meredith and tell

her what was going on, but she'd known better. Faking her death had been foolish and Meredith would never understand. Nor would Meredith have approved of what Valerie had become—the mother of two psychopathic mutants who used their mental powers to destroy others.

A few minutes later Valerie was in the bathroom down the hall, vomiting.

She thought of herself as the strong one, but she wasn't. Thinking about Candelmas and Perpetual Light always left her shaken and sick. That was why she took so many pills. To make memories hazy; to dull pain.

She was weak when she came back from the bathroom; weak, and she slept.

III

A SMIRK touched the taxi driver's mouth. "Yeah?"

"I'm going to Wayland."

"Long ways."

"I'm willing to pay."

The cabbie shrugged. "Hop in."

At ten o'clock, the airport was a depressing place, the seats filled with dozing people waiting for the next flight, grubby children who wouldn't behave, and ragged old men who looked like molesters. A black man in a green uniform swept snow from the area around the cab stand. A beautiful woman got into a new emerald-green Lincoln.

Emily got in the back seat of the cab. Sandra leaned in and said, "Will you wait here, then? I wanted to get you before you left. I need to make a phone call."

The cabbie shrugged again.

"I'll be right back."

As she made her way back into the terminal, she saw that another plane was just landing, a DC-10 reflecting runway lights and snow as it taxied toward the airport.

She had to hurry.

Cordair couldn't be far behind.

She found a phone booth, closed the door, and dialled

the number that was never far from her mind.

WHEN THE CALL came, Tyler was squirting some cheese on a Ritz cracker and watching a rerun of *Mr Ed*. Tyler was nineteen years old, had read Joyce, Tolstoy, and Eliot and spoke three languages. *Mr Ed* was one of his guilty pleasures.

Before answering it, Tyler glanced up the long stairs leading to the second floor of this old rambling frame house. Valerie was up there but she wouldn't be getting it, not after the seizure she'd had this afternoon.

Pushing himself up from the couch, his open copy of *People* magazine sliding from his lap (he hadn't realised that Sally Field looked quite so good in a bathing suit), he hobbled over to the phone and snatched up the receiver.

"Hello?"

"It's me."

"God, I was starting to worry."

"You're sweet, Tyler." She paused. "Emily's with me."

"Where are you?"

"At the airport. Just about to get a cab and come to the house. But…" She hesitated. "You're so goddamned innocent, Tyler."

"God, I wish you'd stop saying that. It makes me feel like I'll never really be a man or something."

"Well, you are, and I appreciate it. Innocence is an admirable quality in this world, Tyler."

"If you say so." He looked around the big living room. The fieldstone fireplace cast a hellish fireglow and deep shadows around the room. The three of them had been meaning to get furniture, but somehow they'd never gotten around to it. He supposed this was because they'd always had to quickly vacate every other place they'd lived. What was the point of buying nice things when you had to leave them behind?

He said, "Something's wrong, isn't it?"

"We may have visitors."

"This means we're going to have to move again, doesn't it?"

"I'm afraid so." Pause. "You know where I keep my gun. The AK-47?"

"God, it always makes me feel like I'm a terrorist or

something."

"Get it, Tyler, and load it and keep it loaded. And keep it very close to you till I get there, do you understand?"

Tyler thought of how it had been in Los Angeles when the government agency had caught up with them; and then in Darien, Connecticut; and then in Green Bay, Wisconsin. Sandra had always grabbed the AK-47, but she'd never actually used it. But one of these times...

"Go upstairs and get my mother ready," Sandra said.

"She won't like it."

"I'm going to give her a shot when I get there and then she won't give a shit one way or the other."

He knew she was getting ready to hang up, so he asked her. "Emily killed some more of them, didn't she?"

"You're better off not knowing."

He smiled bitterly. "Keep my innocence intact?"

"Something like that, yes. See you in a bit." She hung up.

It was never easy waking Valerie up.

As usual, he had to go into the bathroom and get a cup of water and run it icy cold and then go in and flick some across her face.

Even in shadow, the only light a dusty golden bar from the hallway falling across the headboard of her unmade bed—even in the dim light it was a mess, something you might expect to find in a college dorm but never in the bedroom of a grown-up woman.

He dipped his fingers into the cup like a priest taking holy water, and bent over and sailed some icy silver drops onto her face.

"Oh, shit, Tyler!" she wailed. "Shit! I asked you not to do that!"

"Sorry, Valerie, but it sounds like we've got some trouble."

She was struggling to come awake. He tried not to notice the breasts moving sumptuously beneath the wrinkled silk of her pink pyjama shirt. She might be a lot older than he was, but that didn't make her any less trouble to him. But she was Sandra's mother and things would just get too weird—as if they weren't weird enough already—if he ever showed any sexual interest in her.

She smelled muskily of sleep and warmth as she let one leg dangle over the floor, dreading the moment when the cold, hard wood would contact the nice warm bottom of her size 7AAA foot.

She held out a hand. Tyler helped her to her feet.

"Is there any coffee?"

"Think so."

"Could you put some on for me?"

"Sure."

She reached up and touched him gently on the side of his face. Her hand was soft and warm immediately. As she raised her arm he saw the luscious shape of her breasts against the silk again. He knew he was going to get a hard-on. He always felt six years old around her.

"I'll go make some right now."

"You're a good boy, Tyler," she said.

Innocent. Good boy. They drove him nuts around this goddamned place. They really did.

Maybe some night he'd slide himself into Valerie's bed and put the moves on her and then he'd see if she thought he was such a good boy.

Wouldn't old Val be surprised when his tongue started flicking over her nipple?

Wouldn't she just go nuts?

He nodded good-bye and went downstairs before he did something really stupid.

Over the next ten minutes Tyler got the AK-47, filled up the Mr Coffee and set it merrily bubbling. Then he dragged one of his big leather suitcases from the hallway closet into his bedroom and started throwing sweaters, jeans, shirts, underwear, socks, and a few dozen of his science fiction paperbacks into a crazy jumble between the two halves of the suitcase.

He was bending over, dropping more socks into the mess, when he heard Valerie's voice behind him. "What's all this?"

He stood up, turned and faced her. "Why don't we go get a cup of coffee?"

Her famous temper was in evidence once more. "Goddammit,

168

Tyler, I'm not a child. Now I want you to tell me what the hell's going on around here." Despite the anger, he could hear the siren of pure fear in her voice. Soon enough, she'd need her medication.

"Let's have some coffee and I'll explain, all right?" He couldn't help himself—this was hardly the moment for glee—but he felt pretty neat about acting like a mature adult. He'd long ago got tired of being treated like a kid. Could he help it he looked like an altar boy?

He went over to her and slid his arm around her. Inside her tan pullover sweater—which did nothing to hide her wonderful breasts—and her designer jeans and red woollen socks, she was trembling.

He led her into the kitchen.

On the way she said, "Sandra called again, right?"

"Right."

"Did she find Emily?" Emily had run away eight weeks ago. Sandra had only found her tonight. "Did Emily get in trouble?"

"If you mean kill somebody, I'm afraid she did, Val. And apparently the government people picked up her trail again, too. That's why I'm packing. Sandra expects them to be here tonight. In which case, we've got to get out of here."

Val started crying then, and it was pretty bad because nobody could cry like Val.

He got her into the kitchen and seated at the table with a cup of steaming coffee in front of her, and then he excused himself and left the kitchen.

He took the stairs two at a time, heading for the upstairs bathroom where all of Val's various medicines were kept.

In the medicine cabinet, he found a hypodermic needle still in its packet. He tore the paper wrapping away, then headed downstairs again.

When he got back to the kitchen, Val had a buff-blue Kleenex going and was blowing her nose with almost comic force.

Tyler didn't say anything, just headed to the refrigerator and rattled around in there till he found the tiny bottle—with the Olin label on it.

He took the needle and inserted it into the rubber end of the bottle. He got 5 ccs into the needle and then went over to Val.

She looked up from her thoughts, startled. "What's that?"

"You know what it is, Val."

"Sandra gives me my medication."

"Sandra isn't here now."

She studied him a long moment, her shining brown eyes and full wry mouth beautiful as ever. "You're enjoying this, aren't you, you little shit?"

"Enjoying what?"

"Playing the big man."

"Maybe it's time you find out that I am a big man." He pumped as much sexual innuendo as he could into the line. He had this fantasy that she knocked the needle from his fingers and came into his arms, her tongue finding a hot home in his mouth.

She giggled. Not laughed. Giggled. "God, Tyler, just stick to copping cheap feels off me, all right? That's sort of cute. But don't try to seduce me because that would just get stupid. Okay?"

He was blushing so badly, even his neck was on fire. He was paralysed, just standing there dopily, the needle in his fingers.

"Here, Tyler," she said, gently taking the needle from him. "Let me do it."

While Tyler stood there, clearing his throat and trying desperately to regain the mantle of his manliness, she took the needle and pricked into a vein on her forearm.

All poor Tyler could do was watch.

V

MEREDITH AND GAGE rented a Chevrolet sedan in Cheyenne and drove the rest of the way.

Despite exhaustion and anxiety about her sister, Meredith still managed to be fascinated by the scenery. She liked the grey hush of dusk.

She had spent most of her life in the flat Midwest, and the sprawling, jagged mountains seemed almost alien to her. In the day's waning light, she could see their snow-topped peaks clearly. A few stars were out by now and lent the jagged peaks an even more exotic aspect.

The rest of the landscape was not as fetching.

The barren, rocky plains, the endless, empty highway, and the twisting, ice-covered creeks suggested a place where life was hard and often lonely.

Occasionally, as they drove toward Wayland, they would see an oil tanker or a pickup truck zoom by in the other lane; even more occasionally they would see a ranch house or cabin lit up against the consuming darkness. But those were the only signs of human habitation. Everything else was rough-hewn landscape.

"You all right?" Gage asked.

"Thanks for asking."

"Is that an answer?"

She reached over and put her hand on his knee. "I can't believe your wife wanted to give you up."

"I can't believe Roger wanted to treat you the way he did."

She laughed. "Two perfectly wonderful people like us dumped on. Isn't that terrible?"

They were silent for a time. The Chevrolet's headlights angled yellow through the night. They were on an empty stretch of asphalt again and Meredith had the fleeting feeling that they were the only two people in the world—sort of like *On the Beach*, one of her favourite novels and movies—just the two of them fleeing through the darkness where monsters dwelt.

"It gets to you, doesn't it?"

"Hmm?"

"The land," Gage said.

She had been staring out the window, thinking idly of Val. "Yes, it does."

"Me, too. I'm used to trees and grass and timber. This is pretty gloomy."

"It's very beautiful, too, it's just—"

"Empty."

As if to refute their observations, a huge semi appeared and nearly knocked them off the road with the wind it stirred.

"Well, not that empty, I guess," he said.

They were in darkness again. Meredith tried to imagine Val

in such a setting. Why hadn't she contacted Meredith to let her know? Why would two sisters who loved each other so much be kept apart?

They saw the town deep in a valley. The dark mountains ringing it gave the impression of a fortress wall.

In the gloom they could see the soft, fuzzy glow of neons against the night. On closer inspection, coming down an endless hill, they saw signs for a McDonald's, a Motel 6, a Pizza Hut, and an Arby's. Among others.

"Hungry?" Gage asked.

"Very."

"Me, too. Want to get checked into a motel first?"

"Why don't we? Then I can take a quick shower before we eat."

He nodded and started looking for a motel.

As they cruised the wide streets, Meredith was struck by how much Wayland resembled a small midwestern town. The only obvious differences were the way the men were dressed—their attire ran to cowboy hats and western shirts and cowboy boots—and the number of horse trailers attached to pickup trucks.

Most of the architecture looked Mexican-influenced, with sandstone and adobe in plentiful evidence. In the residential areas the houses ran to small, one-storey frame places that suggested a frugal and very serious lifestyle with no frills. The exceptions were a couple of stately Victorians that rambled across rather large estates. Every town of any size had its rich people.

All the locally owned motels reminded Meredith of the Bates Motel in *Psycho*—which Gage laughed about at length—so they chose the Motel 6.

Once they were in the room, Meredith unpacked her bag. Gage planned to buy some fresh clothes in the morning. He went to the TV and dialled around until he found Toni Brokaw. "Can't help it," he said. "I'm a news junkie."

"I'll hurry as fast as I can so we can go stuff ourselves."

Gage patted his small beer belly. "Yeah, like that's what I really need. To stuff myself some more."

She leaned over and gave his belly a playful pat. "I don't care what anybody says, I think pregnant men are cute."

And before he could fire a crack back at her, she gave him a quick but tender kiss on the lips.

Meredith was in the hot shower, slathering soap on her body, before it struck her: She was spending the night in a motel with a man she did not know all that well. Or rather, a man she hadn't known for very long. In fact, she felt she knew Gage quite well by now, at least on an intuitive basis. And that was why she felt comfortable, she supposed. She didn't have any sense of 'shacking up,' or any sense of shyness or awkwardness, which even after a few years she'd still felt with Roger. She felt at home with Gage.

She dried her hair and towelled off.

She'd brought a fresh bra, blouse, panties, argyle socks, and jeans in with her. She finished dressing in the bathroom, ran a comb through her hair again, and then went out to tell Gage that she apologised for taking a little longer than she'd planned but that she was now ready to go.

But Gage wasn't there.

The only gas station Gage could find open was one of the convenience stores so common now in western states.

A beefy kid in a UNIVERSITY OF WYOMING sweatshirt was behind the counter talking to a grey-haired man in a khaki fatigue cap. The man smoked his cigarette as if he'd never heard of lung cancer.

Behind the counter, a TV set with a nine-inch screen played M*A*S*H, with smirky Alan Alda pontificating on why he was right and the rest of the universe wrong.

"Excuse me," Gage said.

He knew he shouldn't do it—that it would have no authority here—but he did it anyway.

"Yeah?" the kid said, irritated about being interrupted. He'd been explaining a complicated pro football play to the older man.

Gage took out his identification, complete with badge, and

showed it to the two men. He knew damned well they'd be impressed.

"I was wondering if you might be able to help me find somebody," Gage said.

"Chicago, huh?" the man said. "That's a hell of a long ways away."

Gage laughed. "It sure is. Especially on a cold night like this one."

The kid was already caught up in the spirit of things, his earlier irritation forgotten. "You want a cup of coffee? It's not as bad as usual."

Gage smiled. "Now there's a recommendation."

The kid got him a cup of coffee.

Then Gage started asking questions.

At first Meredith thought he might be playing a trick on her. Without thinking, she went over to the walk-in closet and peeked inside. Gage's single-breasted tweed topcoat hung there.

Next, she went over to the door. The chain lock had been slipped off.

She opened the door and looked up and down the hall. A heavyset man who looked like a salesman was coming down the hall under the weight of three huge sample cases. He smiled at her and nodded just as he stopped at his room.

She smiled back and closed the door.

Gage had gotten thirsty and gone to look for a Diet Pepsi. He'd forgotten something in the car and had gone to get it. He'd gotten tired of the stuffy room and gone for a walk in the chilly western night.

Gage might be doing any of these perfectly harmless, perfectly safe things.

She would be foolish to get all worried and excited. Gage was, after all, a police detective. He could take care of himself. He was also, she felt sure, as attached to her by this time as she was to him. He wasn't going to run out and leave her.

Besides, his winter coat was hanging in the closet.

She went over and sat down in a chair, watching the rest of

174

the evening news while she waited for Gage to come back.

Everything was fine... perfectly fine. There was nothing to worry about... absolutely nothing.

Meredith was repeating these things to herself a few minutes later when the door opened and Gage walked in.

"I may have gotten us a lead," he said.

But right now, feeling like a deserted child, she didn't care about leads or anything else.

She drew him into her arms and just held on tight, making sure he wouldn't get away ever again.

VI

AT THE SAME TIME Gage was reappearing in the motel room, Candelmas was stepping off the Learjet on a dark and windy airstrip seven and a half miles due west of Wayland. The white Cessna seemed almost phosphorescent in the gloom.

His bulk covered by a black camel's-hair topcoat, his head covered by a vast European-style homburg, Candelmas stood on the edge of the strip watching a new black Buick four-door make its way up the concrete toward him. Voigt, his driver, had made arrangements for a car as well as for a fashionable house that was on a time-share arrangement. The house was vacant for the next three weeks. Voigt paid for two weeks in cash.

Voigt pulled up next to Candelmas, who promptly got inside. He moved quickly and gracefully for a man his size.

Voigt spent ten minutes transferring several bags from the plane to the Buick. As always, Candelmas had brought an estimable amount of luggage.

Inside the car, Candelmas said, "We should have brought Ellen Frazier. She's good at finding people."

Voigt said nothing. Just drove the car. Voigt waved to the owner of the small airstrip. The man, fascinated, waved back. Everybody was fascinated with Candelmas. He could simply have been just one more rich, fat man. But there was some grand air about him—you met people like Candelmas only once or twice in a lifetime. Even if you felt leery of such men, you were drawn to them, too, because they seemed almost like representatives of another, and superior, species.

The Buick shot away from the airstrip.

"I should have brought Ellen."

Most times, Candelmas spoke to himself. He neither wanted nor expected an answer.

Voigt seemed to sense that this was a different occasion. "She couldn't have made the trip, sir."

"No?"

"She was too weak."

"How do you know that?"

"While you were in the bathroom I took her pulse."

"I see."

"Not in good shape."

"Then I'm glad I got a doctor up to the room."

Voigt looked over at him. "It seems to wear them down, doesn't it?"

"Did I ask for your opinion, Mr Voigt?"

Voigt said nothing. Just drove. The night was black. The Buick hummed almost monotonously.

"You didn't answer my question," Candelmas said.

"No, you didn't ask for my opinion."

"Good. Then I trust you'll keep it to yourself from now on."

Voigt said nothing.

"Is that correct?"

"Yessir, that's correct."

"Thank you, Mr Voigt."

Candelmas stared out the window. A lone coyote ran along the edge of the road and was momentarily blinded by the headlights, swinging its long head to the right. The coyote vanished quickly in the darkness.

The drive took half an hour. Voigt seemed to know exactly where he was going. He was very good at planning and at detail. He found out everything he could in advance.

The Buick turned right on to a short, dusty road. Voigt went half a mile at top speed and then turned right again, this time into a driveway.

The house was native stone and wood, a sprawling ranch-style that sat on the edge of a creek that shone icy silver in the

176

moonlight.

Voigt gave Candelmas the key to the house and got out to start unloading the car.

Candelmas went inside.

The place managed to smell both cold and stuffy. Faint traces of cigarette smoke irritated him. Why, when all the facts were known, did so many people still persist in smoking?

The house was nicely appointed in a slightly self-conscious, western-style way. Large moose antlers were displayed above the mantel of the huge stone fireplace; leather furniture covered with festive Mexican blankets filled the living room; and to the right of the dining room table was a large mural of a battle between red men and cavalry soldiers.

Candelmas snagged his bottle of Drambuie from Voigt as his driver toted in all the bags. Candelmas rarely went anywhere without his Drambuie. He found clean glasses in a cupboard above the dishwasher and poured himself a liberal dose.

He went down the hallway and found the den and went in and turned on the TV. He needed to relax tonight. He found an old episode of *The Honeymooners*. He'd always vaguely had a crush on Audrey Meadows anyway.

After a while, Voigt appeared in the doorway. He'd turned up the heat—you could hear it shuddering through the sheet metal ducts—and he'd made Candelmas a ham sandwich from some food bought along the way. Candelmas took it from him, nodded his thanks, and started watching TV again. Ed Norton was going through an especially funny bit and Candelmas was roaring. He never tired of Ed Norton, never.

Voigt, nodding silently as if in salute, withdrew from the den and returned to the kitchen.

He lifted the phone with pantomime exaggeration, angling his head to the hallway so he could see anybody coming, and dialled the number he'd been given.

Voigt whispered, "It's me."

"Where are you?"

"In the house. For the night."

"How's it going?"

"Good. He's ready to start looking for her."

"I need you to keep me posted on everything."

"I know. And I plan to, Mr Cordair."

And with that, Cordair hung up.

What a strange man, Voigt thought. What a strange man; in his way, just as strange as Candelmas himself.

VII

THE MEN HE'D MET at the convenience store had given Gage two different addresses to check out. Both fit Gage's description of places where strangers had settled over the past year or so—strangers who pretty much kept to themselves.

The first place was a farmhouse six miles east of town.

As they drove, Meredith put her head back and closed her eyes. Ever since she'd seen Valerie's sweater, a glowing image of her sister kept appearing in her mind.

Now more than ever she believed that her sister was alive, and that they would soon be reunited.

"Here it is."

"It looks deserted."

"Lights are just off."

Gage rolled the rental car down the dark, rutted driveway leading up to a grubby farmhouse that looked as if it hadn't been fixed up since the Depression.

A dog that looked like a combination of German shepherd and mutt lunged off the porch and started jumping up and down in the snow-flecked beams of the headlights.

"God, he really looks vicious," Meredith said.

Gage nodded. "Wait here."

"Aren't you afraid of him?"

Gage reached over and patted her hand. "Of course. But we don't want him to know that, do we?"

Gage got out.

The dog was on him immediately, throwing himself into Gage's stomach and legs.

She was amazed to see how easily, and knowingly, Gage calmed the animal down.

Standing in the headlights, Gage began petting and stroking

178

the dog so skilfully that the animal was soon whimpering good-naturedly.

Gage went up on the porch.

He was on the third step when Meredith saw something silver glint in the peripheral glow of the headlights.

Then Gage was walking backward, one step at a time, until he reached the ground. He held his arms up in the air.

An old man with white hair, a corncob pipe, and bib overalls held a double-barrelled shotgun to Gage's forehead.

Meredith couldn't hear what they were saying to each other.

She slammed off the heat button.

She still couldn't hear.

The man poked Gage a couple of times with the shotgun.

Gage made no move to look like a hero.

The man finally took the gun away from Gage's forehead and then waggled it in the direction of the car.

Gage, still holding his hands up, walked back to the driver's door and opened it.

"Now you get in your goddamned car and leave me the hell alone," the old man said. "If my two sons 'n' me want to keep to ourselves, that's our business."

Gage got in the car, shut the door, pulled the gear lever down into reverse, and started backing out of the drive.

"God," Meredith said, excited and still trembling. "Weren't you afraid?"

Gage glanced over at her and grinned. "But I didn't want him to know it."

"I take it that wasn't the house we were looking for."

Gage smiled. "I guess not. Maybe we'd better try the other one."

Then Meredith noticed Gage's hands on the steering wheel. They were shaking.

VIII

SANDRA AND EMILY arrived an hour after Sandra's phone call.

Sandra said nothing to Tyler as she came into the living room from the front porch—an irritating habit she'd developed over the years—stamped snow from her feet and then started up the stairs to the second floor.

Emily stood in the centre of the room, mute and frightened.

Sandra paused on the stairs, one gloved hand on the banister.

"Come on, Emily, let's see Mother." They climbed to the top of the stairs.

Tyler watched them. He couldn't help but smile. It was good to see Emily again.

When Sandra opened the door, she found Val on the bed, fully dressed, a magazine draped across her chest, her lips puckered with silent snoring. Obviously, Tyler had given Val her shot.

Sandra took off her coat, laid it neatly across the bed, and went over to the closets, where she began to pack both her bags. She figured they had two, three hours at most before Cordair got there and killed them.

Emily sat on the edge of the bed, letting her mother hug and stroke her as if she were a very small girl. Emily had always been the most troubled of Val's children—tormented, brilliant, terrified of so many things, a mutation of all Perpetual Light supposedly stood for, a creature out of Poe.

As Sandra finished the packing, she said, "How're you doing, Emily?" She could see her sister sliding into one of her depressive moods.

"Fine," Emily said in barely a whisper.

Sandra and her mother glanced at each other. Poor Emily.

Sandra went over and sat between the two of them on the bed.

"I'm so happy to be sitting here with you," Sandra said.

"I just wish we had time to enjoy all this," Val said.

Sandra nodded. "I know. But it won't be long before that man…"

"Cordair?" Val said.

"Yes."

"I can't imagine why anybody would be so obsessed with us."

Sandra almost smiled. Her mother still hadn't figured out

180

who Cordair was. Candelmas's Law, as it had come to be known, was almost always true: *The Truth Ends at Forty*. For some reason nobody had ever been able to explain, most psi powers had gone by the time a person reached his or her fourth decade. The Russians had been trying to extend the term but had had no luck at all. They'd been working on it for sixty years.

Sandra took her mother's hand... held it gently. "You may see your husband tonight." Sandra had never been able to call Candelmas 'my father.' Never. "Are you strong enough?"

"Oh, yes. I'd never go back to him."

Sandra could easily have monitored her mother's thoughts, but she wanted to grant the woman as much privacy as possible. She leaned over and kissed her once more with a sweetness and honour that was particularly feminine, that no man could ever really understand.

As she watched all this silently, Emily thought of Cordair out there somewhere in the darkness.

She would confront him sometime tonight; she was sure of it.

By then, of course, her mother would know just who Cordair was and just what he wanted.

There was a good chance that the knowledge would kill her.

Emily also knew that her mother would somehow see Meredith tonight, too. Emily had left enough clues in Chicago to lead Meredith here. Despite her mother's wishes, Emily felt that the two sisters should be reunited before it was too late.

And then she thought of Cordair again. She had long prided herself on her psi powers—but she wasn't sure that she could handle Cordair. He just might be the ultimate specimen her father had so long dreamed of.

IX

VOIGT KNEW it was Cordair. Who else could it be in the boonies this way?

Candelmas was in the other part of the house, still watching TV. He did most of his thinking this way, parked in front of a boob tube, one part of his mind on the screen, the other on his

181

problems.

Voigt went up to the front-room curtains, parted them, looked out.

On the slight incline to the west of the house sat a GM sedan of some kind (who could tell them apart these days?). The lights were on. Voigt could see nothing beyond the dark windshield. The wind was so strong, the car shook slightly.

Voigt had the sense he was being watched. Cordair always gave him that feeling. Ever since the man had contacted him four months ago with a nice cash offer to keep Cordair fully informed of Candlemas's comings and goings, Voigt had sensed that he was dealing with one really spooky son of a bitch. Candlemas was plenty spooky; Cordair was even more so. The guy wore all the right clothes and said all the right things, but glance at his blue eyes sometime when he didn't think you were looking and you saw—

—death. There was no other way to explain it. An absence of human life. What else could you call it but death?

The sedan pulled over to the shoulder of the road. The lights went out. Then the driver's door opened and for a moment there was a flash of dome light. Then the door closed and everything was dark again.

For the first few minutes Voigt couldn't even see Cordair coming down the edge of the road.

Definitely spooky shit with this guy, Voigt thought.

There he was.

Running along the edge of the road.

Trench coat flapping against his legs.

Running down the edge of the driveway now.

Crouching the closer he got to the house.

Cordair stepped to his right, glanced over his shoulder at the TV room, and then leaned in and opened the front door. Easy. Real fucking easy.

Voigt wasn't sure what Cordair was going to do here tonight, but he assumed that Cordair didn't want his presence known to Candlemas. Not at first anyway.

Cordair slid sideways through the door, smelling of Brut and wind and cold.

182

"Cold, huh?" Voigt said.

Cordair gave him one of those death looks. "Yeah. Cold." Both men spoke in whispers. Cordair nodded to the rear of the house. "He's back there, huh?"

"Right. You want me to go get him?"

"I'll do it."

"What do you want me to do?"

He had never seen Cordair smile before. His smile was hideous.

Voigt opened his mouth to speak again and it was right then that Cordair killed him. "I just want you to die, fuck-face," he hissed. "Just die."

It took very little. Cordair reached up, made his fingers into a 'v' shape, placed their tips to Voigt's forehead, and Voigt pitched forward making a hell of a lot more noise than Cordair had expected or wanted.

Cordair froze, waiting for the sound of the television down the hall to quell, and for Candelmas to ask if everything was all right out there.

But the TV volume remained at the same level and Candelmas made no extra noise whatsoever.

Cordair, pushing his hands deep into his trench coat pockets, started walking slowly down the hall.

Goddamn, but he loved Ed Norton. Oh, Candelmas loved the Great One, Jackie Gleason, too, but he had a special affection for Norton the sewer worker, because in a world of selfish, corrupt people Ed was a true innocent. He fitted the world Candelmas had long ago hoped to create through telepathy— a trusting, giving world where individual destiny took back seat to collective destiny, with mankind not only going to the stars but making the stars a better place. Ed Norton might not be a genius, but he was pure-hearted and for Candelmas that was more than enough.

Ed was just now sitting down to play the piano, cracking his knuckles and doing all his other preparatory work that so infuriated the impatient Ralph Kramden. "Will you get on with it?" Kramden shouted, and of course Ed jumped a little at Ralph's booming voice and his sweet-sad Irish face seemed, as always, a tad wounded by Ralph's rage.

Somebody was in the house.

Though his formal telepathic powers had long ago deserted him, he had enough of a residue left to act as a burglar alarm.

Somebody was in the house.

And it wasn't Voigt.

Candelmas reached over and picked up the forty-five he always kept near him. He then reached up and snapped off the table lamp. The only illumination was the black-and-white glow of the TV, which reminded him of the 1950s, before there was colour.

He picked up the remote control. He brought the TV volume way down.

At first, all he could hear was the furnace blowing softly, steadily through the air ducts.

He eased himself up from his chair.

Somebody was in the house and he was standing outside the door to the den.

Candelmas decided to surprise his guest.

When the man came through the door, there Candelmas would be, forty-five in hand, like a figure on an old pulp fiction magazine.

For all his idealism, Candelmas had no compunction about killing other people in certain circumstances. In certain circumstances, there were a lot of people who probably should be killed.

The door eased open slowly. The furnace continued to blow soft hot air through the house. Behind Candelmas, the audience was roaring about something that Ralph had just said to Trixie.

The door came all the way open now and there stood a tall, handsome, very military-looking young man in a Burberry trench coat complete with epaulets.

Suddenly, Candelmas had a jarring, overpowering sense of who this young man really was.

But before Candelmas could quite complete the thought, the young man stepped into the darkened TV room and said, "Good evening, Father. You probably thought I was dead by now."

There was nothing pleasant about Cordair's smile; nothing

pleasant at all.

X

HE'D ONCE BOUGHT one of those Time-Life books on handy-dandy auto repair, but as with most things mechanical, Tyler had screwed things up pretty badly.

The first thing he'd tried to fix was the fuel pump, which was a little like a first year pre-med student trying to perform brain surgery. A little beyond his present capabilities, despite all the handsome illustrations he had as a guide.

Tyler had had no idea just how many parts constituted a fuel pump, or how difficult they were to put back together once they'd been spread out over a table.

He'd ended up mooching twenty-five dollars off Sandra so a tow truck could come get the infernal beast of a five-year-old Pontiac station wagon they'd been driving the past three years.

He'd handed the tow truck guy the fuel pump—rattling around inside a brown paper lunchbag.

The tow truck guy had smiled a very superior smile and said, "Thanks a lot, Chief," making Tyler feel even younger and more inept than he was.

Tyler thought of all these things as he stood out in the hard-blasting cold night and loaded all the bags into the wagon.

He supposed it was sexist, but no matter how often Val and Sandra said they'd 'cut their belongings down to nothing,' there were at least one or two additional bags each time they had to move hurriedly.

He kept loading, thankful for the exercise in this bitter cold.

When he was finished loading, he'd start up the car and see if everything sounded right. Twenty minutes ago, Sandra had said that she wanted to be a fourth of the way to Los Angeles by dawn.

Which meant the car would have to be running pretty goddamn good.

Which meant that Tyler was going to have to get the beast started up and listen for any potential trouble.

Though he was charged with maintaining the car in case they needed it in just such an emergency, could Tyler's judgement really be trusted?

What if they got up into the mountains and the car gave out?

They'd never trust him with anything again; they barely trusted him now.

Which didn't exactly improve his self-image.

He continued throwing bags into the back of the Pontiac. At least he was good at mule work. Everybody had to be good at something.

After he closed the lid, he turned around for his nightly gaze at the stars and the mountain passes below. He always jokingly referred to this as his 'religious experience for the day.' The odd thing was, staring up at the sprawl of stars across the heavens, gazing down into the deep passes and ravines of the snowpeaked mountains, he did feel closer to God. He had no real idea of who or what God was, of course, but it didn't matter because bathed in the starlight he felt a kinship with forces nobody could name anyway. They were simply too vast and different from anything humankind presently understood.

He wished, too, that he could be more like Sandra and Val. Though he was born of parents gifted with psi powers, none of these powers had ever been his. He showed no trace whatsoever of ESP abilities.

After a time, the wind chafing his face, he turned to go back inside.

Which was when he saw the car coming up the angling mountain pass that wound right past this place.

Something was wrong; he sensed it instantly.

He had to get back inside and warn Val and Sandra.

Maybe this was the night the government people would finally catch up with them after all.

XI

"THERE IT IS."

"I'm scared," she said. "Of seeing my sister again, I mean."

"We don't even know if it's the right place yet."

"From what you said, the people at the convenience store said there were only two possibilities."

"Maybe neither possibility is right."

"Yes, but somehow I think it's them."

Gage reached over and patted her hand. "Mind if I say something?"

"What?"

"That you're likely to be disappointed."

"You really don't think it's them?"

"This is the kind of country where people come to hide out. For a lot of reasons." He laughed. "That's why God made mountains."

"So people could hide out in them?"

"Exactly."

The heat was making her groggy. The rental car seemed to be one of those sleek new vehicles that had everything but a heater you could adjust. It was either too hot or too cold.

"I'll pull up here and go to the door." The house was two stories. Lights had been burning on the second floor. They suddenly went out. Now no lights shone at all, anywhere.

"Looks like they don't want any company," Meredith said.

"I guess not." Gage pointed to a Pontiac station wagon. In the wind, it rocked from side to side. "Look in the back."

Meredith squinted, saw the shape of suitcases and flight bags. "Going somewhere."

"Why don't you go up to the front door?" Gage said. "I'll go around back."

"You're serious?"

"Sure." He patted her hand. "I'm a cop, remember? We're supposed to do stuff like this."

XII

A FEW MINUTES later, they got out of the car.

By now, the night was freezing. Icy wind rattled dead trees and wailed like sorrow in the mountains. Electric poles swayed in the gloom, their light dim and muzzy.

Common as the house was—a two-storey affair of clapboard and stone—there was a sinister quality to the curtain-drawn windows and the closed doors.

Meredith had no doubt this was the right place. "Do you

187

believe in vibes?" she said.

"Sure. A cop has to. It's another word for premonition. And I definitely believe in that."

He leaned over, kissed her on the cheek. "Let's get it over with."

They both started out on the long, narrow walk, but halfway down, Gage crouched and took off running to the right. He had soon vanished around the edge of the large house.

As she approached the front door, Meredith tried to listen for any sounds coming from inside, but all she could hear was the wind ringing in her ears.

She was aware of the arc of bright stars overhead and wished she could pause a moment to look at them.

But then she remembered Valerie. She walked faster.

There was a small brass knocker in the centre of the door. She used it three times. It made a feeble tinny sound against the wind.

She didn't really expect an answer, not with all the lights being suddenly killed, and she didn't get one.

She next tried the small glowing disc of the doorbell. As she pressed it she put her ear to the door, listening for the doorbell sound inside.

Fruity chimes broke the interior stillness; the noise was unexpected and almost comic.

By now, the wind was rough on her nose and cheeks and fingers, and her bladder was getting positively demonic.

She wondered what Gage was doing.

There was a small, screened-in back porch that had been locked with a latch.

In moments, Gage had his trusty pocket-knife out and flipped the latch up and went inside.

Summer lawn furniture was stored back here, along with two garbage cans that smelled faintly of sweet rot. He could see into the kitchen through a wide window with ruffled curtains.

The place was orderly and empty.

The inner door took a lot more work.

Gage always carried a small set of burglar tools he'd lifted off a particularly inept second-storey man one fine spring evening along the shores of Lake Michigan. The guy had been a two-time loser, yet he'd strolled along the lake, obviously casing some of the high-rise condos and dreaming the creamy dreams of cat burglars everywhere. The man was now in Joliet.

Gage got to work. He could taste sweat on his upper lip and feel sweat soak his armpits. Being a burglar definitely took a certain kind of courage.

At the front of the house Meredith shivered in the darkness. She was thinking about going back to the car and getting warm for a few minutes when she suddenly heard, sharp as gunfire on the wind, the sounds of people shouting angrily at each other.

She tried the front door. Locked—no good.

So she ran around the west side of the house, following Gage's snowy footsteps all the way around to the back.

She found the rear porch. From the kitchen, a light shone. She could see the back of Gage's head and shoulders. He had his arms up in the air, something somebody had obviously ordered him to do.

Meredith crept up on the porch as quietly as possible, keeping low and constantly scanning the kitchen window for sight of another face.

A woman began talking, then. Quickly, angrily.

Valerie?

Meredith's heart pumped furiously; could it really be this simple? Just walk through the kitchen door and find her sister?

But then the woman moved into the frame of the ruffled curtains and Meredith got a clear look at her.

The same woman who had been following her all over Chicago, the woman with the head scarf and dark glasses, both of which she wore now.

XIII

CANDELMAS sat in the big leather recliner and looked on the face of his son. He hadn't seen him in many years. He couldn't believe that a freckle-faced boy, so uncertain of himself, could possibly grow into this tall, strong, harsh man.

"You know why I'm here," Cordair said.

"I'm afraid I don't."

"I'm going to kill you."

"I see."

For the first time, Cordair smiled. "You wouldn't give me that pleasure, would you?"

"What pleasure?"

"Of seeing you frightened."

Candelmas thought a moment and then smiled, too. "I suppose that's just what I was doing, wasn't it?" The smile left abruptly. "But then you could always monitor me and find that inside I'm terrified of dying, just like anybody else."

Cordair stared at him. Anger was apparent in both his gaze and his voice. "You should have checked into what your co-workers were doing."

Candelmas nodded. "I only found out about it later."

"There was a lot of sexual abuse."

Candelmas's face became grim. "You?"

Cordair nodded. "They were a sweet goddamned bunch, Father, your scientists."

"Most of them were good people."

"Most of them, maybe. But the rotten ones more than made up for the others."

"That was the problem with losing my psi powers as I got older. I couldn't monitor anybody to find out what was really going on."

"They'd learned about blocks by then, anyway. It wouldn't have mattered."

Candelmas indicated the Drambuie on the stand next to the recliner. "Care for a drink?"

"No."

"Mind if I have one?"

"Since when did you care about my wishes?"

Candelmas's mouth was touched by a sad smile. "Self-pity doesn't become anybody, Richard. And believe me, I know. I've felt sorry for myself since the day I was born." He nodded to the decanter again. "Now why don't you have a goddamn drink with me?"

Cordair shook his head.

Candelmas poured himself a drink.

After taking a healthy sip, he said, "I imagine you'll kill me first and then your sisters, correct?"

Cordair said nothing.

"That was always the thing I feared," Candelmas said. "The person with the most psi ability wanting to rule everything, be the only one."

"I don't worry about anybody except Emily. She has some exceptional talents." He smiled. "But I'm the ultimate specimen, Father. I'm the dream you had."

For a long moment, Candelmas just stared at him.

"So now you're going to murder your sister?" Candelmas looked at Cordair in disbelief. Not until this exact moment had he truly understood that the young man was insane.

"You should be proud of me. I have powers you haven't even dreamt of yet, Father."

"Oh, yes," Candelmas said, staring into his snifter and then taking another drink. "I'm very proud of my children. My daughter runs all over the country murdering everybody associated with Perpetual Light, and now my son wants to be some kind of goddamned roadshow Superman. After killing his own sisters, that is."

"Not Superman, Father; not yet. There are still many things I can't do. I had to use very conventional methods to track everybody down. Someday I'll be able to track people through my psi resources."

Candelmas stared at the boy a long time. His eyes filled suddenly with tears. "I started all this crazy shit, didn't I?"

Cordair just watched him.

"Me and my goddamned dreams. A better species. World peace. All my crazy bullshit."

By now, Candelmas was crying openly. "And what did I produce? Two insane children who kill people."

Cordair, clearly not impressed, said, "You're right about one thing, Father. Self-pity really doesn't become you."

He didn't wait for his father to respond.

He raised his hand, pointed at the TV set with a single finger, and then jerked his head to the right almost imperceptibly.

Instinctively, Candelmas's own abilities rose in him. He pointed a finger at Cordair, and the man was slammed into the wall.

He looked more startled than hurt.

And as he came off the wall, he laughed. "You've never quite lost your abilities, have you, Father? I'm impressed."

But this time Cordair gave Candelmas no chance at all. He swung his head in the direction of the television.

The TV set exploded into flame and shattering glass.

"How am I doing, Father? Are you suitably impressed with your prodigal son?"

Cordair moved his finger quickly around the room.

The drapes burst into fire. The bookshelves became smoking rubble. The walls began to race with flames.

Candelmas tried to rise from his chair, but Cordair had set up some kind of force field, some invisible wall Candelmas couldn't penetrate.

"Now for my final trick of the evening, Father," Cordair said.

And then he turned back to his stunned father, who was still trying to push out of the leather recliner.

Cordair set the arms of the chair afire.

"It's getting hot in here, isn't it, Father?"

Then Cordair set a circle of flame in motion so that the chair was entirely surrounded.

"Good-bye, Father."

And then, with a single gesture, Cordair set the entire chair aflame.

Candelmas's screams were lurid in the heat and fire.

"Please, please help me, Son," Candelmas called out as the fire began to snap at his clothes. He sounded like a young boy.

"Good-bye, Father," Cordair said.

He took a final look at his father there in the burning chair. The screams were getting worse.

Then Cordair turned and left the room, walking through the fire without hesitation.

Only one thing remained now; dealing with his sisters. And then Cordair would be supreme.

He walked outside and back to his car.

3

I

TYLER SAW HER FIRST.

He had walked into the kitchen—she could hear the heavy tromping of his boots—and then he'd peeked out the window and seen her standing there on the porch.

Her natural inclination was to flee, of course.

It was a terrible thing to leave Gage there, but how could she help him if she, too, were captured?

She pulled up out of her crouch and started to run down the steps of the porch, but Tyler was too quick for her.

He grabbed her hard by the shoulder and spun her around. In that instant, he looked like a tough if slightly gangly young man, but his voice spoiled the whole effect. "You'd better come inside or Sandra's going to be pissed."

His words made it clear that the woman named Sandra was in charge.

Meredith saw there was no use in resisting.

"I don't want to hurt you, ma'am."

She wrestled free of his grasp. "I can walk in on my own. I don't need you touching me."

She could see that she'd hurt his feelings by saying this; she almost smiled. He really should give up the tough-guy act. It just didn't become him.

She looked inside and saw Gage glancing over his shoulder at her. He shook his head, silently saying that there was no use resisting.

She pushed past the young man and went inside. Meredith looked over at Gage. "Are you all right?"

"So far," Gage said.

"Stand over by him," the woman said. She held a gun.

"What're you going to do?" the young man said.

"I'm handling this, Tyler."

"But, Sandra—"

She waved the gun and Meredith moved across the tiled floor. To Tyler, she said, "Bring the big gun down here. We'll probably need it."

Tyler nodded and trotted out of the room. Meredith was trying to figure out what was going on, but as yet it was hopeless.

The kitchen was warm and bright and clean. Several new appliances shone on the countertops.

Sandra said, "There's somebody who wants to see you."

Meredith's head snapped around. "What?"

"You heard what I said. And you know who I mean." Then, "You don't know this yet but you're my aunt."

"Your aunt?"

"Yes," Sandra said. "And your sister's upstairs with my sister Emily."

Sandra dropped the gun she'd been holding into the pocket of her coat and came across the room and abruptly took Meredith in her arms. "My mother will explain everything," she said. "In the meantime, I need to talk to your friend here about helping us. We need to keep packing the car. We have to get out of here."

But Meredith was no longer hearing the words. Her mind played the sentence *And your sister's upstairs,* over and over.

Valerie. Alive. Upstairs.

She felt curiously immobilised.

"Valerie is still alive?" was all Meredith could say.

"She's still alive," Sandra said. She nodded to Gage. "I wasn't sure who he was till I saw you." She squeezed Meredith's hand. "Come on. You'll want to see Valerie."

Just then Tyler reappeared in the kitchen. He carried a huge, ugly automatic rifle, one Meredith recognised as the terrorists used.

"Give me the gun, Tyler, then you can show Meredith upstairs."

Tyler handed Sandra the gun.

Meredith glanced at Gage. She could see his eyes smiling; he was happy for her. She wondered if she looked silly, tearing up the way she was right now.

Suddenly everything looked so wonderful; a Technicolor happy ending. She could imagine sunbeams splashing through the ruffled white curtains and the smells of bacon and eggs and hot coffee on the air, and a robin sitting on the windowsill.

She started crying openly now, and she didn't care at all.

She left the kitchen and followed Tyler through the dark house, up a steep staircase, and into the room where her sister waited.

She had waited so many years for this; so many years.

II

JUST BEFORE his eyes came open, Candelmas heard somebody shouting. He thought of his mother and then of Valerie and then of his beautiful teacher Mrs Craig. But it was none of them.

Heat. Smoke. Lashing yellow flames.

The shouting continued.

A man; but who? And what did he want?

Then Candelmas realised that the shouts came from two different voices, one of them his own...

The other man's name was Ken Dodge, a grain-elevator operator who'd been driving home from a 4-H meeting and seen the rental house on fire.

Being a good man, Dodge had pulled his pickup into the driveway and jumped out, prepared to rush into the flames to see if anybody was in there. A car was parked in the driveway—there was a good chance somebody had been caught in the blaze.

It looked funny—theatrical, like a movie stunt. The sky and mountains and grasslands were dark and there in the middle of it all was this small house completely engulfed in flames, fire snapping and crackling in long fingers at the stars, and waves of punishing heat moving up the driveway.

Dodge heard the shouts as soon as he jumped down from the cab of his truck.

In response, and not thinking a moment about his own safety—he'd been just this silly back in Korea when an enemy sniper had shoulder-shot him for going out to haul back a wounded GI—he whipped off his leather jacket and held it up over his face as a shield and ran right into the burning house.

The first thing that happened was that he nearly tripped over a body just inside the front door.

With all the smoke and fire and heat, he had to bend down to look at the man. Nobody he knew. The man was dressed in some kind of chauffeur's uniform or some damned thing like that. Who the hell in these parts had a chauffeur?

More shouts.

Dodge took one more look at the guy on the floor and wondered what had killed him. Not the fire, that was for sure. Where the chauffeured had eyes, there were now only two bloody holes. It was as if his eyeballs had exploded from their sockets. Thick blood was splattered all over the man's face.

Dodge realised yelling would do no good. The fire made enormous noise; the walls and ceilings were starting to cave in and crash to the floor in ragged fiery chunks. This only increased the noise and made hearing the other man all the more difficult.

All Dodge could do was run room to room and peek inside. For the first time—the whole roof starting to make cracking noises—he thought of his own well-being. If anything happened to him, his wife would never get over it. She was that kind of plain and simple person; that kind of loyal. Just the same kind of person Dodge was.

Ten feet ahead of him a door was flung back and from it emerged a huge man dressed all in black. Smoke rose from his clothes. Even in these circumstances, the man suggested incredible charisma and strength.

He was coughing so badly, his entire body shook.

Just as the man's knees started to give way, Dodge reached across and grabbed his arms, but the man weighed too much

196

and collapsed to the floor before Dodge could catch him.

Dodge realised that they both had only minutes to live, minutes before the smoke filled their lungs or the rest of the ceiling fell in.

He leaned in and started shaking the man. "You got to get up, mister, you got to!"

Above the roar of the fire, Dodge could hear his own sobbing, both from smoke and from frustration.

"Come on, mister! Hurry!"

The man's eyes flew open suddenly. There in the fiery light, Dodge had the impression that he was staring at a man who had just come back to life. "Hurry, mister, otherwise we're gonna die!"

Dodge could see that the man had suddenly begun to understand their situation.

He leaned forward, surprisingly spry for someone his size, and began the difficult process of getting to his feet.

Frantically, Dodge scrambled to his own feet and then gave Candelmas a hand.

Toward the rear of the house, the rest of the ceiling fell in.

"Hurry, mister! Hurry!" Dodge shouted.

They were six steps from the front walk when the closest part of the roof collapsed and brought most of the house down with it.

"How you doing, mister?" Dodge asked ten minutes later.

Candelmas lay sprawled on the brown winter grass near the car Voigt had rented for them. His breath was still coming in ragged spasms, but he was finally able to focus on the moment and figure out everything that had happened.

As soon as he remembered Cordair, he remembered that his daughters' lives were in jeopardy. He had to find them, and soon.

"I need to get this car going," Candelmas said.

The ease with which he sat up and got to his feet obviously surprised Dodge. You didn't often see men of Candelmas's size who could move around so easily.

Candelmas walked over to the rental car, opened the door, and looked inside. He had no interest whatsoever in the burning house behind him.

The keys weren't in the car. He hadn't thought they'd be, but it had been worth a try.

When he walked over to Dodge, he said, "Do you know anything about cars?"

But Dodge wasn't interested in cars at the moment. He stood staring at the blazing house as if it were a movie screen. Without taking his eyes off the collapsing timbers, he said, "Did you know that there's a man in there, mister?"

"I know."

"Wore some kind of chauffeur's uniform."

"Right."

The heat was still coming in lapping waves from the house. Dodge said, "I'd better go call the fire department."

"Can you help me with the car first?"

"Help you how?"

From his back pocket, Candelmas took out his wallet.

Candelmas took out two one-hundred-dollar bills and said, "I'm in a hurry. I need you to hot-wire that car."

For the first time, Ken Dodge seemed suspicious about everything that had gone on tonight. "Mister, I think maybe you'd better stick around and talk to the sheriff."

Candelmas laid the two hundred dollars in Dodge's open palm. He said, "My daughters' lives are at stake here. I really need your help." He paused. "Please."

Dodge looked reluctant for a moment or two longer, then he shrugged and went over to the rental car.

Dodge wouldn't have made much money as a car thief His method was clumsy and lengthy and consisted mostly of trial and error, but finally he got the job done.

He even shot Candelmas a toothy, boyish grin of triumph when the car roared into life.

Candelmas leaned in and said, "Do you know most of the people in this area?"

"Most of them, sure."

"I'm looking for a house where a woman and two or three younger people might be living."

"Younger people?"

198

"Late teens; early twenties."

Dodge thought a moment. Candelmas tried to hide his impatience. "Could be a couple of places. You should ask at Abner's."

"Who's Abner?"

"Abner himself is dead but his tavern's still in town."

Dodge then described how to get there.

"Thank you," Candelmas said as Dodge came out of the car and Candelmas slid in behind the wheel.

"Sheriff's probably not going to be happy you didn't stick around," Dodge said.

But by now, Candelmas couldn't hear anything. He had the big car in reverse and was backing out of the driveway.

III

MEREDITH HAD ALWAYS imagined that when the time came when she finally walked into a room and saw that Valerie was alive and well, she would run to her older sister and throw her arms around her and hug her until both of them began to shake joyously with tears and laughter.

But it was not that way at all, for either of them.

Tyler led her up the stairs, flipping on a light only when they reached the second-floor landing. Then he led her down a long, narrow corridor with closed doors on both sides; finally to the very end of the hallway, where he rapped twice on a door with one knuckle, almost like the tattoo of a code.

"Come in," a faint female voice said.

Tyler nodded for Meredith to follow.

Meredith's stomach began to knot up as it often did at times of high stress. All she could think of was that she wished she had some Maalox.

Tyler opened the door and then stepped back for Meredith to come inside. Tyler the doorman.

A slight woman with ash-blonde hair, wearing a man's blue V-neck sweater and a pair of wheat jeans and a pair of argyle socks sat in the middle of a big mussed waterbed smoking a filter cigarette. She flicked the ashes into a presumably empty

199

Diet Pepsi can.

She was, of course, Valerie; and she was not Valerie at all.

"This is pretty weird, isn't it?" the woman said. She had a quick but very melancholy smile.

Meredith, panicked, glanced over at Tyler.

Tyler said, "It's really her, Meredith. It's really your sister."

Valerie said, "I wish I could have told you all about this back in our Perpetual Light days, Meredith. But I couldn't. I really couldn't."

Even from here, Meredith could see that Valerie's small hands were trembling. It had the curious effect of making Meredith like this woman for the first time since coming into the room. Her daughter Emily sat in the corner unmoving.

"God," Meredith said, "It really is you."

The sad smile again. "It really is." She dropped the cigarette in the pop can, set the pop can on the floor, and then held out her arms. "Why don't you come over here and sit down with me? That way it'll be easier to cry and hug and do all that stuff that Tyler is expecting to see."

Tyler laughed. "Yeah. Just like on the tube."

"C'mon, Meredith. Come here."

So Meredith went, not quickly at first, because a strange paralysis seemed to have come over her again. Her steps were oddly halting, like those of a person just learning how to walk again after a terrible accident.

But gradually, the steps led her to the bed and she bent over and let Valerie take her in her arms and pull her down to the bed and—

And then they both started doing just what Tyler had expected all along.

Wailing and blubbering and squeezing and holding each other at arm's length for an oh-my-God-let-me-look-at-you and then going back to the wailing and the blubbering and the squeezing and the holding each other.

"Why didn't you ever tell me the truth?" Meredith said. "I spent so many nights wondering if—"

Valerie leaned forward and tenderly dried one of Meredith's tears with a small, clean handkerchief Then she glanced significantly over at Tyler. "Would you mind leaving us alone?"

Tyler grinned. "Actually, I kind of wanted to hear this. Sort of like a soap opera, only for real."

"Isn't he a charmer?" Valerie said.

Tyler, happy for them both, nodded good-bye and found his way downstairs, where he joined Gage and Sandra in loading up the station wagon.

Before long, they'd have to be leaving.

IV

IT WAS EASY to imagine the town of Wayland as it must have been at the turn of the century. Most of the buildings would have been false fronts, the streets would have been nothing more than dirt that a water wagon sprayed down in the hot, dusty months and that ice caked in winter. A small, noisy frontier town tucked up at the base of a sprawling mountain range.

But it was very different now.

Against the snowy night stood the beacons of commerce in bold, bright neon: McDonald's, Burger King, Pizza Hut, National Video. And more.

He drove slowly down the main street, looking for the place that Dodge had mentioned.

He drove some more, turned a corner, and found himself on what appeared to be an entire block of taverns.

Even in the stinging snow and whining wind, he could hear the war of jukeboxes and the high, hard sound of men laughing. Here and there a drunk weaved his way through the neon glow down the dark street. Here and there lovers paused to fumble with each other in the gloom and chill. Here and there a drunk leaned against a tree pissing a steaming yellow stream into a snowbank, thinking in his alcoholic stupor that he was somehow invisible.

Candelmas found a parking space and pulled in. His lungs and throat were still raw from the smoke. His clothes reeked of the stuff, too.

He got out, straightened himself up, took clean, cold air into his lungs, and then walked across the street toward the noise of a Willie Nelson song.

Even from here, he could smell the yeast and barley of beer, and the oppressive stench of cigarette smoke.

The moment he opened the door, three-dozen heads turned to him and glared. It was as if they were all animals recognising some supernal enemy.

He knew how he must look—he'd always been able to objectify himself—huge and imposing and dramatic. In cities, he looked eccentric. In hick towns, he looked even odder; suspiciously odd. He found all this amusing.

"Well, Jesus Christ," said one of the tavern toughs, "What is it anyway?"

He got all the expected laughter from his friends.

For a moment Candelmas wanted to turn around and go back. Why suffer these assholes anyway? Surely in this town there were other places, other people he could go to. But then he stopped himself. He didn't have much time.

Candelmas made his way up to the bar.

The men were of various sizes and shapes, though they seemed to have three things in common: Their eyes were glassy with alcohol, they all seemed in need of a shave, and they all wore caps of different kinds and colours, though caps bearing the name of agricultural products seemed to be the most popular.

"Jack Daniel's, if you've got it," Candelmas said, "On the rocks."

Candelmas's voice startled most of the onlookers. He had a great booming theatre voice, one that could easily reach the last row of playgoers or, in this case, shitkickers.

His voice obviously gave some of the gawkers pause. It suggested, in its depth and resonance, both intelligence and superiority. No lisp; no whine. Nothing they could easily make fun of.

The bartender glanced around anxiously—as if getting permission from his customers to serve Candelmas —and then shoved both of his arms beneath the bar and came up with a fifth of Jack Daniel's. He dropped some cubes into a glass, splashed the whiskey over the rocks, and gave Candelmas his drink.

Candelmas laid a crisp new twenty on the bar. "I'll probably have another drink or two. You keep that for now."

With that, Candelmas turned around and looked to the back of the bar where two booths stood empty.

He picked up his drink and walked back there. Despite the rush to find the house where Valerie was staying, Candelmas knew he needed the drink; the fire had nearly killed him.

He was just sitting down when one of the men pushed away from the bar and came up to him. He wore a down vest, a chequered shirt, a chin six days shy of a shave, and some of the worst body odour Candelmas had ever encountered. He had a crescent-shaped scar on his right cheek and one of his front teeth was missing. He worked hard at acting tough.

"I don't think you should sit down there, mister."

"No?" Candelmas said. "And why would that be?"

"Cause we don't allow people like you to drink with men like us."

"Well, I'm sorry to hear that."

And without any macho ceremony, Candelmas's right hand shot out and grabbed the man by his neck.

With his other hand, Candelmas calmly set his drink down on the table.

Then he turned around and began choking the man even harder, lifting him up off his feet in the process.

He shook him as if he were going to tear his head from his shoulders. The man's arms flailed madly, and his feet kicked to reach the floor.

"I don't like you," Candelmas said. "And I want you to leave me alone. Do you understand me?"

Candelmas could see that the man would soon be dead. But he was getting just enough pleasure from this to keep it up for a few more seconds.

The man's eyes frogged out; he tried to speak. He kept flailing and kicking.

His buddies started pleading with Candelmas to put him down; please, mister.

But instead of putting the man down, Candelmas flung him

back into the bar so that he cracked the middle of his spine hard against the edge, and then crumpled to his feet, his hands grasping for his throat.

Candelmas sat down and resumed sipping his drink.

A few men helped the fallen man, but the others just stood there sneaking looks at Candelmas, who reasoned that he'd probably just made himself a few friends in this place. Doubtless the man who'd accosted him had been a bully who'd picked fights with many of them. Everybody loves to see a bully get his.

Candelmas took more of his drink.

When his second drink was delivered by an infinitely more respectful bartender, Candelmas said, "Do any of these men deliver mail?"

"Huh?"

"Do any of these men deliver the mail around here? I need somebody who knows the area on the outskirts of town."

"Frank Hardy ain't a mailman but he did the census last year."

"Would you send him over here'?"

"If he'll come."

The bartender went to the far end of the bar, right in front of the door, and interrupted a conversation three men were having. He beckoned to one of them and then nodded to Candelmas. The man said something Candelmas couldn't hear. The man's two companions smirked and kind of shoved their friend playfully. Then the man shrugged as if to say what the hell, and walked over to Candelmas.

The man was tall and angular and worn. He was probably thirty but looked forty-five. "You want to talk to me?"

"You took the census?"

"Yep. But so what?"

"I'm looking for somebody. I thought maybe you could help me find her."

"What if I don't want to?"

"Oh, you'll want to," Candelmas said. From inside his pocket he took three crisp hundred-dollar bills and put them on the table, right next to where the man stood. "Can you see the denomination? It's pretty dark in here."

"Guess I can't."

"Pick it up. Look at it for yourself."

The man did so. "What kind of fuckin' gag is this, mister?"

"No gag at all. I'm looking for information and I'm willing to pay for it."

"You'll pay three hundred dollars for information?"

"That I will, son."

Candelmas could see the man clicking off all the ways he could spend the three hundred. The man wore a wedding band. If he was a good man, then he'd been thinking of all the ways he could spend his money on his family.

"There ain't no catch?"

"No catch."

"I give you the information and you give me the three hundred?"

"That's right."

"This is the goddamnedest thing I ever heard of."

"Yes," Candelmas said, "I suppose it is."

Then he proceeded to ask the man about the information he needed.

V

IN THE KITCHEN, Sandra was showing Gage how the AK-47 worked. She handled the automatic weapon with the fixed wooden butt and the thirty-round box magazine with almost theatrical ease, handing it over to Gage after she'd explained that it fired three to four hundred rounds per minute at a cyclic rate. Earlier, she had explained to him who they all were—Valerie, Emily, Tyler, and Candelmas.

Now, she handed Gage the weapon.

Gage took the weapon, examined it, and said, "Who're we expecting. The Communists?"

Sandra laughed. "No; my brother, Cordair."

"You expect him to be that violent?"

"Very violent. He wants to kill me. He wants to kill us all, in fact." Then she told Gage about her powers—and about

Cordair's.

Gage hefted the weapon. "Exactly what am I supposed to do with this?"

"I'd like to station you at the front window, if you wouldn't mind."

"And when I see him... ?"

Tyler came through just then. He didn't read the mood in the kitchen at all right. He said, "Man, they're having a great time upstairs."

"... You kill him," Sandra said.

"Kill him? Just like that?" Gage said.

"Kill who? What're you two talking about?" Tyler wanted to know.

"Because if you don't kill him, he'll kill all of us. Including Meredith. Believe me."

"I wish I knew what you two were talking about," Tyler said.

"Oh, yes," Sandra said, leading Gage back through the house to the darkened living room. "I'd like you to keep Tyler with you."

"Keep me with him?" Tyler said. "For what?"

"To protect him." She reached up and patted Tyler gently on the cheek. "He's pretty obnoxious but I'd hate to see anything happen to him."

"Hey," Tyler said, following them into the living room. "That isn't funny at all."

VI

HE STOOD on the downsloping side of a foothill, field glasses held to his eyes, gazing into the shadows moving about inside the house. He'd even managed to get a glimpse of the assault rifle Sandra had been showing Gage in the kitchen.

A great weariness overcame him then, an emptiness he could not understand but only suffer. It was not an unfamiliar feeling and sometimes he wondered if it sprang from the fact that he was the only one. Sandra had powers, to be sure, and over the course of Perpetual Light, there had been others who showed an enormous range of psi skills as well. But he was the only one who truly represented a breakthrough, the next step in evolution that his father had so long sought and dreamed of.

There were men in Germany who had taken up his father's old dreams and made new ones from them, and Cordair would go there when he was finished tonight. They would help him become even more powerful; and together they would help define the future of mankind.

But Cordair wondered if any of this would fill the hollowness he felt at such moments as these.

He took the field glasses down, and sighed.

He knew what he wanted to do, and soon enough it would be over.

He started walking across the shadowy ground separating the foothills from the house. He wanted it over with now; these were the only people who knew about him—Emily had conveniently enough killed all the others for him—he wanted it over with and he wanted to be gone, create a new identity for himself, and a new species for mankind.

In his way, he was as much a dreamer as his father.

He began by destroying the station wagon sitting in the driveway.

VII

"I USED TO daydream about calling you."

"Really?"

"Umm-hmm. Especially after I left Candelmas. I just had the children and I was on the run and I was so scared and I—"

"I wish you would have called me."

"I know. And I'm so sorry I didn't, Meredith. I really am."

"I'm just glad we're together again."

They were still in the bedroom; still on the bed.

"Things will be better now," Meredith said. "You'll see." Then she looked over at Emily. Valerie explained how Emily had tried to bring the two sisters together.

"I'm afraid," Valerie said. "All the time—just afraid."

And just then they heard steps pounding up the stairs and Sandra shouting, "Cordair's up on the hill. I just saw him."

207

She started to say something else, but her words were drowned out in the terrible concussion that rocked the entire house.

VIII

THE EXPLOSION shook the house like a bomb blast. Safety glass and metal and plastic slapped against the picture window, yellow flames and dark debris hurled high into the night.

On the other side of the fire stood Cordair, watching them. Gage knew now just what sort of powers the man had. For the first time, the AK-47 looked puny in his hands.

Sandra crouched next to Gage, looking out at the fire as it crackled in the darkness.

She tapped the assault rifle. "I guess this isn't going to do much good."

"Maybe we should call the police."

Sandra smiled. "We can't afford the publicity, Gage. And anyway, they couldn't stop my brother."

As if on cue, Cordair raised his right hand and pointed it in the direction of the house.

The glass of the picture window imploded. For several long, sickening moments the air was filled with pieces of silver glass, both large and small, thrown into the living room like spears.

One such shard caught Gage directly in the chest.

He screamed and fell backward, the AK-47 failing from his hands and sliding across the hardwood floor.

In the darkness, given eerie flickering shadows by the fire in the driveway, Sandra crawled over to him on her hands and knees.

But before she could even examine him, she heard a small gasp from the staircase and saw Meredith rushing over.

"Keep down!" Sandra said.

Meredith dropped to a crouch and duck-walked over to where Gage lay bleeding and moaning.

"We have to pull the glass out," Sandra said. She looked up and saw Tyler, terrified, watching. "Get some rags from the kitchen."

He went without a word, probably happy that he didn't have to look at Gage anymore.

Meredith pressed her face tenderly to Gage's and touched long fingers to his face.

In the flickering shadows, pain was obvious on his handsome features. She could smell blood and sweat and urine.

Tyler was back in moments.

Sandra started to take the rags, but Meredith said, "Let me do it, Sandra."

Meredith worked quickly.

She wrapped the rags carefully around the end of the glass she would use as the hilt and then slowly began pulling the glass from Gage's chest.

He moaned even louder now.

"I'm sorry," she told him, then glanced at Sandra as if for approval to proceed.

Sandra nodded.

Gage continued to moan. Biting her lip, knowing the additional pain she was causing the man, Meredith whispered a prayer to herself and resumed inching the glass from Gage's chest.

"Go get all the gauze and bandages you can find," Sandra said to Tyler.

Tyler nodded and left again, a shadow lost among other shadows.

The night wind through the shattered front window was harsh and keening and cold.

Gage started trembling.

"Just a little bit longer," Meredith said, fighting tears.

And it was then that the front door was blown away as if by a grenade, the door ripping from its hinges and flying across the room and smashing into the fireplace.

Silhouetted in the doorway, the yellow-red flames of the car explosion flickering behind him, stood Cordair.

Sandra jumped to her feet, turning abruptly to face her brother, when Tyler came back into the room, hands filled with cartons of gauze and bandages.

Cordair raised his hand. A moment later Tyler was screaming, dropping the items he'd been carrying. He looked to Sandra, as if pleading for help, but it was too late because his head began to collapse in on itself. There was no other way to describe it. His head began shrinking and folding, his brains pouring from the folds and splashing down on his shoulders and chest. Finally, Tyler pitched forward to the floor.

Meredith had finished pulling the glass from Gage's chest and was hovering over him protectively.

Peripherally, she was able to see what happened next.

Sandra faced Cordair squarely now, raised her own hand, and pointed it directly at him.

Where the air had been chill moments before, great invisible waves of heat moved through the remains of the living room now.

Meredith saw that Cordair looked both terrified and completely startled—as if this should not be happening.

Sandra moved in, closer, like a fighter closing for the kill.

She raised her hand again.

This time a slash appeared across Cordair's forehead. As blood began pouring across his face, Cordair's scream drowned out all other sounds.

She continued walking in closer, closer.

The next time she raised and pointed her hand, blood began pouring from Cordair's right eye.

Meredith glanced up to see Valerie on the staircase now, watching her daughter and son try to destroy each other. Emily was right behind her.

Cordair surprised Meredith by pushing away from the wall and raising his own hand.

Sandra's arm fell away from her torso; blood trickled, then splashed down the side of her body.

Emily stepped in front of her, facing Cordair, and then started walking toward him.

While Meredith could not see the beams of power that passed between them, she could see the effects of these invisible weapons.

Every few moments Emily would jerk violently, as if powerful volts of electricity had just passed through her.

Every few moments Cordair would moan as pain jolted his body.

Valerie came running down from her place on the stairs, shrieking for both of them to stop.

She tried to fling herself at them but was blown back away from the roaring wind that now encircled her son and daughter. The two moved closer together.

Soon they met in the centre of the living room, two battered, dying psychic warriors. Glass and debris flew through the air; wind wailed; Meredith clung to Gage; and Valerie lay sprawled next to Tyler, sobbing.

Cordair grasped Emily's shoulders and dug his fingers into her flesh and bone so that his power could be transmitted easily throughout her body.

She pressed the fingers of her right arm into his forehead.

And then the icy blue light began.

They had created some kind of force field around them and now the entire house began to quake, as if it would soon collapse in on itself.

Within the perfect capsule of pure energy they had created for themselves, Emily and Cordair began to systematically destroy each other.

Off came Emily's arm, blood gushing from the hole; Cordair's nose was ripped away, only a bloody hole remaining.

By now they had formed a terrible symbiosis, ineluctably linked as they were destroyed.

The wind was ripping off the wainscoting; the icy blue light was blinding.

And within it, Emily and Cordair alike cried out in their dying moments.

Shortly the wind began to lessen; then, as their cries began to fade, the icy blue glow grew dim. The two figures collapsed.

Now on the floor lay the remains of two animals that had once been people with minds and spirits and souls. In the doorway, silhouetted against the car fire outside, stood a huge man dressed in black.

He had been watching the final moments of Emily and Cordair's battle, knowing there had been nothing he could do, knowing their struggle had been inevitable.

Now he came slowly into the room, looking first at the terrible remains of the dead brother and sister on the floor, and then at Meredith and Gage across the room and at Valerie sitting over by them, weeping.

He walked toward Valerie, an imposing figure even amidst all the clamour and sorrow. When he reached her, he bent over and extended a huge hand, and, helping her to her feet, took her into a deep embrace. He held Valerie as both a father and a lover, and let her weep in his arms until she was so drained that all he could do was pick her up and take her upstairs.

IX

THROUGH THE LONG NIGHT, police cars, ambulances, and even two fire trucks came and went, their emergency lights painting the ragged foothills blood-red.

The police tried to act as if they saw this sort of thing every day—carnage, automatic weapons, a house that looked as if it had literally been bombed—but every once in a while one of them started shaking his head as if in a daze, or giving a little involuntary shudder, or saying to one of the survivors, "Now tell me again, just what the hell happened here anyway?" They sounded as young and scared as kids.

Meredith stayed behind for a time to talk to the police. Clearly, they realised that there were many things she was withholding from them, but knew they were in way over their heads. Federal authorities would get involved, they told one another. Perhaps the federal boys, who prided themselves on being so smart, might eventually have better luck sorting all this out.

Finally, just before dawn, sharing their third thermos of steaming black coffee with her, the police let her ride into town with a neighbour. Her boyfriend Gage was in the hospital there.

Meredith stood by Gage's bed. "Is it all right if I say I love you?"

Gage grinned. "Fine by me."

"How about you?"

"How about me?"

212

"Do you want to say that to me?"

From his white hospital bed, where he was propped up so he could see the new blue sky in his window, Gage laughed and said, "Yeah, I guess I do." Then he paused and put out his hand and she took it and he said, "I love you."

She leaned over and kissed him and then she started crying. He asked her what the tears were about and she said she wasn't sure.

And that was the hell of it; she really wasn't sure at all.

Later that morning, after the doctors had come and gone, assuring them both that Gage would be fine, he finally asked, "Where're Valerie and Candelmas?"

Meredith looked out the window. "Gone. They didn't want to be around to answer any questions."

Then she looked down and shook her head. "I may never see her again, Gage. Ever."

He took her in his arms and held her, tighter than he should have, given his pain, feeling the grief that he knew would never leave her, no matter how much he loved and protected her. No matter how much.

IV

SOMETIMES HE was late but that didn't bother her. Being a cop wasn't like being a magazine editor. Nobody ever said that cops had regular hours. And she'd better get used to it. In four months, they would be married.

It was spring in Chicago, which was why she was sitting in the soft, warm apple blossom breeze of an outdoor cafe, one of those stagey little bistros that tried hard to effect the ambience of a Paris sidewalk.

In front of her on the table was a buff blue envelope addressed to her in a lovely, painstaking hand.

Valerie had always been so proud of her handwriting.

And then Gage was there, a scent of maleness and after-shave, a quick dry kiss on her cheek and a gentle squeeze of her hand. And pure wonderful love in his blue gaze. The same pure wonderful love that could be found in her own hazel gaze.

She nodded at the letter. "Val," she said.

"How're they doing?"

She shrugged. "She said she found out that she'd never really quit being in love with him."

He looked at her carefully. "Well, that's good, isn't it?"

"Yes. I guess, anyway."

"Then why the hesitation?"

She tapped a red nail against the buff blue envelope. "She's pregnant."

"God. Really?"

"Really."

"But isn't that good news?"

She raised her hazel eyes and looked across the table at Gage. A red-jacketed waiter was coming over to them now. She wanted to enjoy this warm spring day and enjoy this man she loved so much.

"You don't think he'd try it again, do you? With their next child, I mean?"

"Oh, God, honey, don't you think he's learned his lesson by now?"

Then the waiter was there, fussing, and an old Supremes song started playing on the jukebox and Meredith saw the season's first monarch butterfly perched on the edge of a nearby empty table.

It was spring and she was truly in love for the first time and what was the use of spoiling it all with her little-girl fears?

Perpetual Light was behind her now; behind them all, really.

Just after the waiter left, she took Gage's hand and said, "I'm so happy, darling. I'm so happy."

And she didn't feel at all self-conscious about her silver tears because they were tears of joy; pure joy.

Val would have another child and everything would be fine; just fine.

Sometimes at night he went up on deck alone and stood looking long hours at the stars, the huge yacht the only vessel anywhere on the water.

214

And Val lay awake in the warm sheets, hand on the swell of her belly, wondering what it was Candelmas thought about when he stood so long looking up at the sky.

And then she would fall gently asleep, the child in her sleeping now, too. Later, Candelmas, tears in his eyes, would slide into bed next to her and lie awake until the boat had drifted from black night into yellow dawn.

He had made such a muck of it; such a goddamned muck.

CT Publishing

If you have enjoyed this book, we are quietly
confident you will enjoy the following titles as well.

ED GORMAN
SERPENT'S KISS

IN A QUIET MIDWESTERN CITY…

…A community is coming apart at the seams. He is a mild-mannered academic turned serial killer being hunted for crimes he doesn't recognise as his own. She is a TV anchorwoman losing the ratings game—and the only person who understands the evil that drives him. Between them, an innocent young girl's life hangs in the balance…

IN AN EMPTY APARTMENT IN THE CITY…

…He has found a manila envelope that holds gruesome photographs of his past deeds and instructions for his next killing. Despite himself, he will follow the instructions as if they were his own will…

IN THE DARK STREET SHADOWS…

…The police scramble furiously to understand him and stop him, while a TV reporter is onto the story of a lifetime. She knows who he is… and who his next victim will be. What she doesn't know is how little time she has left—and how terrible is the power of the Serpent's Kiss…

Price: £4.99 ISBN: 1-902002-09-1
Available from all good bookshops, or post free from:
**CT Publishing, PO Box 5880,
Birmingham B16 8JF**
www.crimetime.co.uk
email ct@crimetime.demon.co.uk

ED GORMAN
NIGHT KILLS

The odd thing was how comfortably she seemed to fit inside there, as if this were a coffin and not a freezer at all. She was completely nude and only now beginning to show signs of the freezing process, ice forming on her arms and face.

But he could tell she hadn't been in here very long because of the smells…

Frank Brolan, successful adman, unwitting fall-guy. Someone has murdered a call girl and planted her in his freezer. Frank has to find the killer before the cops find him.

As the body count rises, with the killer leaving Frank's mark at every crime, Frank flees into the night and the city. He finds help in an unlikely duo—a teenage whore and a wheelchair-bound dwarf with a mind like a steel trap...

"A painfully powerful and personal novel about three outsiders— an alcoholic advertising executive, a man twisted and disfigured by spina bifida, and a runaway teenage girl—brought together in a noir unlike any you've ever read. Violent, melancholy, bitterly humorous, Night Kills is a 'relationship' novel of the classic mould. As disturbing and sad a crime novel as I've ever read."

—CEMETERY DANCE

Price: £4.99 ISBN: 1-902002-03-2
Available from all good bookshops, or post free from:
CT Publishing, PO Box 5880,
Birmingham B16 8JF
www.crimetime.co.uk
email ct@crimetime.demon.co.uk

ED GORMAN
CAGE OF NIGHT

TWENTY-ONE-YEAR-old Spence returns to his hometown after two years in the Army and falls in love with Cindy Brasher, Homecoming Queen and town goddess to a long line of jealous men. A string of robberies put Spence at odds with his obsessive love for Cindy. One by one Spence's rivals are implicated in horrific crimes. Spence wonders how much Cindy knows, and why she wants him, like her past boyfriends, to visit the old well in the woods...

"The book is full of Gorman's characteristic virtues as a writer: sympathy, humour, commitment to the craft of storytelling, and a headlong narrative drive. A real writer is at work here and there aren't many of those to go around."

—DARK ECHO.

"Cornell Woolrich would have enjoyed Cage Of Night."

—LOCUS.

"A book that combines romance, sex, violence, madness and an almost oppressive degree of grief, Cage Of Night is one of the most unique noirs ever written."

—PIRATE WRITINGS.

"Gorman is defining noir for the nineties."

—CEMETERY DANCE.

Price: £4.99 ISBN: 1-902002-02-4

Available from all good bookshops, or post free from:
CT Publishing, PO Box 5880,
Birmingham B16 8JF
www.crimetime.co.uk
email ct@crimetime.demon.co.uk

GWENDOLINE BUTLER

A NAMELESS COFFIN

Nobody took much notice when the handbag slashing began in London. A few women found small nicks in their handbags, others huge gashes. John Coffin had a feeling that the cases were going to lead to something far more unpleasant. A similar case in Scotland—of coats, this time—comes to trial in Murreinhead, and Giles Almond, a mild-mannered officer of the Court, is viciously attacked by a knife-wielding assailant.

Then the body of a missing Murreinhead woman is discovered in a rotting tenement in London, and the chase is on...

Coffin's investigation moves between the two locales and suspense builds as yet another murder victim is discovered...Where is the killer? And what is the connection between London and Murreinhead?

'[Butler's] inventiveness never seems to flag; and the singular atmosphere of her books, compounded of jauntiness and menace, remains undiminished'

—PATRICIA CRAIG, TLS

Price: £4.99 ISBN: 1-902002-11-3
Available from all good bookshops, or post free from:
CT Publishing, PO Box 5880,
Birmingham B16 8JF
www.crimetime.co.uk
email ct@crimetime.demon.co.uk

GWENDOLINE BUTLER
COFFIN   IN   OXFORD

"It was like a Chinese puzzle. In St Ebbe's was a flat, in the flat was a trunk, and in the trunk was a body. The body of a woman..."

Ted was brought round from the first attack, if you could call it an attack, with difficulty. He had been found shut up in a cupboard with a scarf tightened around his neck: his own scarf, to add insult to injury...

'Gwendoline Butler is excellent on the bizarre fantasies of other people's lives and on modern paranoia overlaying old secrets; and her plots have the rare ability to shock'
—ANDREW TAYLOR, THE INDEPENDENT

ISBN: 1-902002-00-8 Price: £4.99

JENNIE MELVILLE
WINDSOR RED

Charmian Daniels, on a sabbatical from the police force takes rooms in Wellington Yard, Windsor near the pottery of Anny, a childhood friend. The rhythm of life in Wellington Yard is disturbed by the disappearance of Anny's daughter with her violent boyfriend. Dismembered limbs from an unidentified body are discovered in a rubbish sack. A child is snatched from its pram. Headless torsos are found outside Windsor.

Are these events connected? And what relationship do they have to the coterie of female criminals that Charmian is 'studying'...? All is resolved in a Grand Guignol climax that will leave the most hardened crime fiction fans gasping.

ISBN: 1-902002-01-6 Price: £4.99

Available from all good bookshops, or post free from:
CT Publishing, PO Box 5880, Birmingham B16 8JF

DO *YOU* HAVE TIME FOR CRIME…?

CRIME TIME

IF YOU HAVE ENJOYED this book you may like to try our quarterly round-up of all that's best in the world of crime fiction. Now in its fourth year, CRIME TIME is acknowledged as the best publication about crime fiction in the world. Interviews, features and reviews mingle with new fiction by some of the world's best writers in a 256 page plus trade paperback format for only £4.99 for a sample copy or £20 for a year's subscription, *plus* a free book.

Recent interviewees and contributors include Ed Gorman, Michelle Spring, Colin Dexter, Mark Timlin, Gwendoline Butler, James Ellroy, Elizabeth George, James Sallis, Patricia Cornwell, Jonathan and Faye Kellerman, Ben Elton, Andrew Klavan, Lauren Henderson, Maxim Jakubowski, Ed McBain, James Patterson, Lawrence Block, Joe R Lansdale and many more.

In addition we have run features, often exclusives, such as Derek Raymond on Ted Lewis, Mike Hodges on making *Get Carter*, a history of Hardboiled fiction, Criminal Cities, featured TV shows such as *Homicide* (with cast interviews) and *The Sweeney*, as well as covering film, radio, audio tapes, video, comics and the theatre.

Why not join in? More reading than the telephone directory of a small town and much more interesting…

Price: £2.99 for a sample issue /
£20 for 4 issues + free book
Available from all good bookshops, or post free from:
**CT Publishing, (Dept EG4) PO Box 5880,
Edgbaston, Birmingham B16 8JF**

www.crimetime.co.uk
email ct@crimetime.demon.co.uk